PRAISE FOR
LORETTA LITTLE LOOKS BACK

"One of my **favorite books** of the year, by far."
—**Jason Reynolds**

"**Complex and evocative**...Sparkling with Southern diction and rhythms, peppered with poems and songs, Pinkney's monologues invite readers' out-loud participation." —*New York Times*

★ "Art adds **elegant portraits of land and family** to these **vivid tales**..." —*Publishers Weekly*, starred review

★ "An **unforgettable reading experience.** Perfect for every library." —*School Library Journal*, starred review

★ "As always, Pinkney's writing **sings, rich with metaphor, lyricism**, and touches of **magic realism**..."
—*Booklist*, starred review

"**A gratifyingly unconventional format** and a musical sequence of storytelling that may **illuminate some stark moments** of our country's history." —*The Bulletin*

LORETTA LITTLE LOOKS BACK

THREE VOICES GO TELL IT

A MONOLOGUE NOVEL

BY ANDREA DAVIS PINKNEY

ILLUSTRATIONS BY BRIAN PINKNEY

LITTLE, BROWN AND COMPANY

New York Boston

Text copyright © 2020 by Andrea Davis Pinkney

Illustrations copyright © 2020 by Brian Pinkney

Cover art copyright © 2020 by Brian Pinkney. Cover design by Jenny Kimura. Cover copyright © 2020 by Hachette Book Group, Inc.

Little, Brown and Company
Hachette Book Group
1290 Avenue of the Americas, New York, NY 10104
Visit us at LBYR.com

Originally published in hardcover and ebook by Little, Brown and Company in September 2020
First Trade Paperback Edition: January 2022

Little, Brown and Company is a division of Hachette Book Group, Inc. The Little, Brown name and logo are trademarks of Hachette Book Group, Inc.

The publisher is not responsible for websites (or their content) that are not owned by the publisher.

Additional photo credits information is on page 264.

The Library of Congress cataloged the hardcover edition as follows:

Names: Pinkney, Andrea Davis, author. | Pinkney, J. Brian, author.
Title: Loretta Little looks back : three voices go tell it : a monologue novel / by Andrea Davis Pinkney ; paintings by Brian Pinkney.
Description: New York : Little, Brown and Company, 2020. | Audience: Ages 8–12. | Summary: Loretta, Roly, and Aggie B. Little relate their Mississippi family's struggles and triumphs from 1927 to 1968 while struggling as sharecroppers, living under Jim Crow, and fighting for Civil Rights.
Identifiers: LCCN 2020005755 | ISBN 9780316536776 (hardcover) | ISBN 9780316536769 (ebook) | ISBN 9780316536790 (ebook other)
Subjects: CYAC: Family life—Mississippi—Fiction. | African Americans—Mississippi—Fiction. | Sharecroppers—Fiction. | Civil rights movements—Fiction. | Mississippi—History—20th century—Fiction.
Classification: LCC PZ7.P6333 Lor 2020 | DDC [Fic]—dc23
LC record available at https://lccn.loc.gov/2020005755

ISBNs: 978-0-316-53673-8 (pbk.), 978-0-316-53676-9 (ebook)

Printed in the United States of America

LSC-C

Printing 1, 2021

FOR GWENNIE

HOW TO READ THIS BOOK

WITH CONVICTION

WITH ATTITUDE

WITH FEELING

WITH FRIENDS

THE LITTLE FAMILY TREE

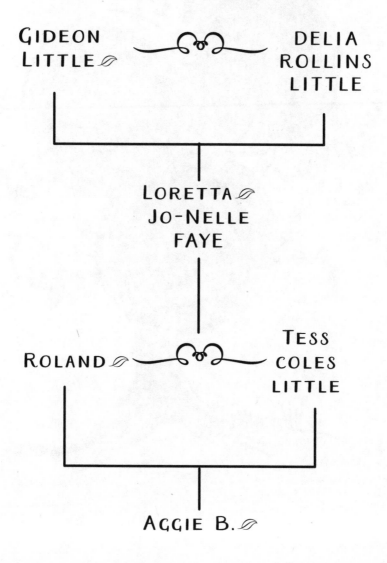

GIDEON LITTLE · DELIA ROLLINS LITTLE

LORETTA JO-NELLE FAYE

ROLAND · TESS COLES LITTLE

AGGIE B.

THE GO-TELL-ITS

BEFORE THE BEFORE

LORETTA 1927 TO 1930

ROLY 1942 TO 1950

BETWEEN THE BETWEEN
PRETTY MISSISSIPPI: A TROUBLED BROTHER'S SOLILOQUY

AGGIE B. 1962 TO 1968

AFTER THE AFTER

BEFORE THE BEFORE

One family, shining bright.

Rising to its firelight.

Three reach back.

     Each a solo storyteller.

One-by-one:

     Recollections.

     Memories.

     Flickers.

     Glimmer-gifts,

enduring—

                 boll weevils

night-deeps

     thorny tests

     doubt

But even in the face of can't-see,

hope lives in the bones

of the Little family tree.

A legacy that begets the go-tell-it of their tale.

     Dawn.

     Slow Sunrise.

     New Day!

LORETTA

1927 to 1930

DAWN

Everything's still.

Blackness.

Until—here comes one bold light. Warming the bare floor.

Enter, Loretta.

She is strong. She is bright. Booming truths, she is.

Loretta's shoulders, straight. Loretta's head, high.

Loretta knows—don't look down when you're looking back.

And don't never back down when it's time to meet memories
face-on.

Loretta's eyes, front. Her gaze, steady.

She is ready.

Prepared to tell it.

S OME SAY, THIS WHAT THEY CALL *ORATION*. I CALL IT truth-talking. Standing up to speak on what-all I remember. Recollecting.

Putting it simple, this is *me* talking to *you*. About my life. About my times. Some pretty. Some ugly.

When I was a child, I got an education in the ways of this world. Wasn't no bigger than a twiglet then. But those sprig-years was what stretched me into full-grown understanding.

And now, I'm coming ahead with a go-tell-it. A story that starts with me, grows out from my family's tree, and ends with you.

Right here, I'm sharing the honest-to-goodness. Me, Loretta. I look back first. Then here come more Littles. Each of us with our own go-tell-it, sharing how it was. Where our feet walked. What-all happened. And the road we're going on, come tomorrow. After we're through, it'll be your turn to speak on what needs to be done for yourself and others when a new day dawns.

Speaking of tomorrow, let me explain to you about *reaching*. Reaching is looking past ugly when it's in front of you, and stretching for a horizon that maybe you can't see today but is out there in tomorrow's wide-open.

Reaching is the space between seeing and stretching.

Reaching is breathing. Seeking.

Reaching is the blood that makes your heart beat for what it wants. So, come with me. With us. Look back.

Reach.

THE BOLL WEEVIL'S BREAKFAST

WHERE AND WHEN: *Holly Ridge, Mississippi.*
September 1927. A wide field of fluffy white,
blooming on the Clem Parker plantation.
Loretta stands front and center.

I T WAS DADDY WHAT FIRST SHOWED ME HOW TO MAKE THE bolls surrender. Said, "Snap from its claw, girl-child. Cotton wants to hang on. Why you think we call it boxing cotton? It's because the boll weevil's breakfast will always put up a fight."

That's right, Daddy taught me everything I needed to know about handling them stubborn plants.

Said, "You gots to fight back. Show that natty stuff how strong you are. Let them boll-weevil beetles go hungry because you snatched away the cotton before they get a chance to feed on it."

Along with Daddy, I lived in a family of sisters, the youngest of three girls. Jo-Nelle and Faye were twins, and much bigger than me, and coming up on their womanhood. They were grown by most counts. Old enough to keep house, work the land, and tell me what to do. Daddy and my sisters showed me the ways of sharecropping. Explained what it meant to be working on Clem Parker's land. I was ten years old.

Daddy, he swore up and down about how slavery had not yet ended, even though Mr. President Lincoln, going by the name of Abraham—same name as the prophet who they call "the believer" in the Bible—took a first step to crush slavery when he issued his Emancipation Proclamation, something near to sixty-five years before. Even though Mr. Lincoln's

Proclamation didn't put a stop to slavery, the president was trying to walk in the direction of slavery's end.

At night, after a day of picking, chopping, and hauling Clem's cotton, *whew*, did my daddy get to cursing. Talking about how the chickens that's running around on Clem's property were more free than we was.

Daddy, night after night, said, "At least those chickens get to keep their feed. Clem don't snatch back their corn after sprinkling it for them to eat."

Daddy, so tired. Daddy, always sick with anger's fever. Daddy, who could never tell Clem how pounding mad he was. And who didn't like to show his temper in front of us children. Still, I could feel the fury rising out from my daddy. So weary about how things was.

Clem, he had a way of irritating people, especially Daddy. He was a landowner whose mouth always twisted into a smile, and who spoke in what sounded all friendly. Smug, was how Daddy described it. When you first met Clem, he seemed sensible. But whenever he voiced Daddy's name, he pulled it out on a long rope, taking his time, and mostly saying it wrong.

Daddy is Gideon Little. How hard is that to pronounce?

But here comes Clem, calling Daddy *Giddyup*, like what you say to make your horse go faster. There was nothing fast about the way Clem dragged it out, though. Day after day, he was deliberate about messing up my father's right name.

"Morning, Giddyup."

"Giddyup, how you doin', how you been?"

"Beautiful day, Giddyup, isn't it?"

To make it worse, Clem would tease out the second part of his mistake for the name Gideon, pulling on the *u*, turning it into a jangly chain of *o*'s.

"We could sure use some rain, Giddy*uuu*p."

"Giddy*uuu*p, I ever tell you how glad I am to know you?"

"A fine person, you are, Giddy*uuu*p. Better than most."

Every time Clem spoke to my father like that, Daddy winced. Bit hard on his lip, same like I do when Jo-Nelle or Faye yanks a comb through my tangled hair after washing it.

Imagine having some slow-talking man who is the boss of you, poking fun at your name all day long.

The strange thing was, even though *Giddyuuup* most times slid off Clem's tongue, he would also go for long stretches of saying Gideon the right way. And he would sing Daddy's praises in front of all of us who worked on his land.

One time, Clem called everyone together, gathered us, and spoke about how hard a worker Gideon Little was.

Clapped Daddy's shoulder. "You see this fine man here?

He's an example of what it means to have integrity and fitness for tending our soil."

On that day, Clem even gave Daddy some bonus pay. A one-time bit of extra money for his good work.

As grateful as we were for those coins, there was something troubling about the way Clem could be. He was confusing. We never knew what to expect.

Daddy said, "That man is like a shiny apple out of season. He looks good on the outside, but you can't be sure if what's beneath the skin is sweet or mealy. It's all a chance."

From when I was a small child, I remember Daddy correcting Clem whenever he bungled his true name. My father spoke firm to his boss, smiled right back, his jaw tight.

"Mister Parker, sir, my name is Gideon, not Giddy*uuup*. And yes, we do need rain. Thank you for the complimentary words about my manner, but can we agree that you will call me Gideon from here on?"

Clem, who must have been hard of hearing, or some kind of tone-deaf, didn't fully honor what Daddy was asking of him.

All he said was, "I appreciate you setting me straight."

One time, when Daddy extended his hand to shake on it, to make a pact, Clem wiped his palms on the thighs of his britches. Kept smiling. Nodded once, but never shook.

After that, he'd respect my father's request for a time, and correctly call him Gideon. But soon Clem would go back to putting his slippery mix-up onto the name Gideon. He'd return to calling Daddy Giddy*uuu*p, pronouncing it as wrong as ever for weeks at a time, followed by more weeks of saying it correctly.

When Giddy*uuu*p spilled from Clem's lips, Daddy, proud, and never shying back from nobody, would firmly repeat, "Mister Parker, sir, my name is *Gideon*, not Giddy*uuu*p."

I once asked my father, "Daddy, how come when you correct Clem about your name, he keeps getting it wrong?"

Daddy thought before speaking. He didn't fully answer what I was asking. I think that had something to do with Clem being an apple out of season, and us never truly knowing what was at his core.

Daddy said, "Child, I only got so much energy. I ain't gon' waste it on a fickle-fool boss, doing what he wants on the whim of whatever way the breeze blows in his one-day-like-this, one-day-like-that way of behaving."

To me, Clem Parker might as well have been pinching Daddy every time he came ahead with his Giddy*uuu*p nonsense. A pinch doesn't hurt that bad once, or twice even. But when somebody keeps nipping you over and over, it starts to eat at your skin. When the pinch comes with a smug smile, the sting brings more pain.

Somewhere along the line, my father stopped correcting Clem. Daddy was still a self-respecting man, but he'd been pinched one too many times. He bore bruises nobody could see. I believe this is what made Daddy so solemn.

When it came to *our* names, Daddy put care and kindness into pronouncing them. Though he and Mama named me Loretta, Daddy always said my name like he was singing a happy salutation.

Left off the *Lo*. Called me *'Retta*, for short. Spoke it like I was royalty. Loved me deep, Daddy did. Loved all us children, while clinging to his memories of Mama.

The truth of it is, Daddy's love was enough to cover what we were missing from not having a mother. Our mama passed soon after I came. People all saying she died of a weak heart brought about by sunstroke, and a disease called sick-and-tired. I was her last baby. Born six whole years after my sisters. Seeing as Faye and Jo-Nelle are older, they have always treated me like I was their child.

When remembering my mother, Daddy said the only thing that ever softened Mama's sick-and-tired was holding me.

Maybe that's why, no matter how hurt or broke-down

Daddy got, he was never too weary to hug us. His arms were more mighty than the feelings he carried around inside. And Daddy always found the strength to sing me to sleep. Hungry blues flowed from his deepest sorrows. Spirituals, too. Songs about sunlight and wading in free waters. Hymns from Daddy's sun-cracked lips, telling how he wanted to be ready to dress in white when heaven called him home.

I believe my love for singing, and for feeling the power of music, is a gift from my father.

In the evenings, Jo-Nelle and Faye rubbed down Daddy's sore back, bent over with the ache of his quiet rage. Can't blame him for being mad. When you're a sharecropper, chickens *do* have more freedom than you. Cows, too. Pigs, even. Dogs, for sure. All kinds of farm creatures got the advantage of doing what comes natural, when and how they want.

Not once did Clem ever pinch at his dogs' dignity, or disrespect any of his farm animals by playing around with their names.

As sharecroppers, we made our living by waking up earlier than early. Had to be ready to work before the *dew* even knew what to *do*, in the dark morning hours we called *can't see*. Had to make our way to fields of blooming white cotton clinging to their prickly thistles.

Spent all day boxing cotton while the sun's blistering hand pressed down hard.

Even though I was the baby of the Little family, when I turned six, I had to work 'longside my sisters. We were forced to give half of what-all we harvested to Clem.

We didn't own not even a snatch of that land. It was Clem Parker's property. In some respects, *we* were Clem's property, too. Not slaves by the law. But enslaved in the spirit. Got spit-pay for the hard work we did.

If we had a bad cropping year, Clem took from our wages to make up for the debt we owed him. Same, but opposite, the more cotton we grew, the more we could keep for ourselves.

Seeing as how I was the smallest of all the kids, and how my fingers were no bigger than twigs, I could get at those cotton bolls quicker than anybody else. So I made a decision. I would do more than *work*. I would *win* in the game of quick picking. I would reach for what I wanted, and nobody would stand in my way.

My first day in the fields was the best and the worst. Clem told me that if I picked thirty pounds of cotton, he would reward me with a bag of cookies. That was the best part—the promise of something sweet I could share with my family. Then came the bad part—the picking!

You ever tried to handle a cotton plant's bur? It is *sharp*. And obstinate. Those burs will hold on as tight as a closed-up fist.

For sure, boxing cotton is a knock-down-drag-out. But I wanted the cookies Clem had promised. And more than that, I wanted to help my family.

In fighting with cotton's claws, I was left with bloody thumbs, ripped skin, and blisters. Cried most of my first day while I picked. Kept on, though. Stayed at it. Reached past the pain. Put all my attention to winning. Would not stop till the other side of *can't see* came back, when the sun had long set, and we worked by the moon's milk. I snatched that thirty pounds of cotton. Yes I did. Saw right away why Daddy was so tired every night.

Clem made good on his word, but only partway. With the picking done, he tossed me a small burlap sack.

"Here's your prize, gal."

This boss man with the easy smile rewarded me with a bag of cookies, like he'd promised, but they were stale gingersnaps, moldy at the edges.

After hours of boxing cotton, all the time thinking on those cookies, my hands and my heart knew what fury feels like.

My sisters did double duty that evening. First slathered

Daddy's back with salve, then dabbed a peppermint-balm mix onto each of my fingers, up and down my arms, and all around my sore ankles and tired feet.

The week after that, I picked forty-seven pounds of cotton. I didn't have to fight with the boll weevil's breakfast, neither. There *was* no fight. I was the nimble winner from the beginning.

CRABGRASS MAD

WHERE AND WHEN: *Holly Ridge, Mississippi.*
Spring 1928. 'Retta stands in a thicket of wild grass,
the ribbon of land just outside her schoolhouse.

P ROUD AS I WAS ABOUT HOW GOOD I COULD WORK COTTON, I was even prouder about being smart in school. I loved learning letters and arithmetic. As far as reading was concerned, I was just as good at words as I was in the fields.

By the time I was eleven, I could unlock a whole peck of sentences from books. I was quick with numbers, too.

I loved school. Every day I marched to that place like I was in a proud parade. Skip-stepped the whole way.

Knees—up.
Head—up.
Eyes—up.

Miss Teacher Lady couldn't help but call on me. My hand was always first, waving high. I was as eager as a croaker in a frog-jumping contest to tell what-all I knew.

Our school was in one room. A tiny shack packed with fifty-and-something kids, from little to big. Boys and girls, all of us Colored. All poor. All hungry to learn what we didn't know, and hard-pressed to get as much of it as we could.

And so, here is a secret I haven't never told. Not a soul knows this. But here, now, I'm gon' speak it out loud.

The day my sisters said I had to quit my schooling, I ran and ran to a far-off field. Buried my whole face in both my thick-skinned hands. Cried and cried like a baby with colic. Got down on my knees and ripped at anything that was coming up from that red dirt staining my skirt. I was crabgrass mad!

I knew this day was coming. *How'd* I know? The same thing had happened to Faye and Jo-Nelle. When you're a share-cropping child, there comes a time when school just ain't practical. When you're a girl like me, who can pick cotton faster than most kids, your family needs you in the fields, full-time. Especially with Mama gone.

All us children knew our time at school would be short, and that the cotton's claws were waiting to pierce the tender skin on the underside of our hands.

At school, we had no pencils or books or paper. We learned by what Miss Teacher Lady wrote on a small chalkboard at the front of that crowded place.

But as measly as our school room was, we bit hard into our lessons. It was as if Miss Teacher Lady had handed out a single ear of corn—that all fifty-and-something of us had to share—and told us to finish off every golden kernel.

We students were neighbors and friends, and we liked each other plenty, but we all wanted that same corn.

You ever seen chickens squabble for a handful of seeds?

You ever seen how pigeons crowd and peck and grab at scraps of bread?

That's what it was like at school. All fifty-and-something of us wanted to gobble up what Miss Teacher Lady was forced to ration because there was only so much to give.

Being sharecropper children, we knew what it meant *to* share. But when your belly is bloated from not having enough, it's hard to be generous or fair to even your best friend.

Boxing cotton is one thing, but snatching at lessons brings on just as much of a fight. It's a tug-of-war for something you can't fully touch. It's not a battle that leaves you with blistered thumbs and cracked skin. It's a fight for wanting to learn reading and numbers.

Like going up against the boll weevil's breakfast, I was winning. I was learning some of the longest words. And I could spell good. I knew how to write my whole name—Loretta Harper Little. I could write Mama's name—Delia. And Daddy's—Gideon. And Jo-Nelle and Faye, too.

I was able to add and subtract from my memory, not even once using my fingers to help me count.

But when it came time to say goodbye to schooling for good, I had all ten fingers wrapped around long blades of crabgrass. I yanked and heaved and hollered out. I understood how my daddy felt having to tamp down what he really wanted to express.

I could sure not ever tell my sisters, or even Daddy, that I was mad for having to quit school. It wasn't their fault. The person to be yelling at was Clem Parker. Aside from him, what truly deserved to be yanked out by the roots was the share-cropping system.

Thankfully, there was one place I could quietly, secretly tell what-all I was feeling. That place was the True Vine Baptist Church, where I attended services with my family. One Sunday, I knelt after the sermon and told the silent air above my head I did not like having to quit school in sixth grade. A band of angels must have been watching down on me, because our choir started to sing a gospel song called "Whisper Wish for What You Want."

So that's just what I did. Without expressing a single word out loud, I wished for what I wanted: to be able to keep up with book-learning and getting educated.

At True Vine, I was no stranger to the choir. Singing with them lifted me to a place I can only describe as cloud nine in a pew. The words of our congregation's hymns carried some kind of special power. My favorite was a simple song. A Christmas hymn that we sang all year, but took it upon ourselves to change the words so that they could suit any Sunday.

The song—"Go Tell It on the Mountain."

Here's one version I recall:

Go tell it on the mountain
O'er the hills and ev'ry where
Go tell it on the mountain
That this new day is born.

At church, like in school, I applied myself to learning. I got to know all the words and notes of as many spirituals as I could. It was as if those petitions went straight to God's ear. Miss Teacher Lady started giving book lessons at church. She taught us to read and study the Bible. I came to see why they call it the *good* book. I memorized every begat and Beatitude that would turn back any bad attitude rising up in me.

SCRAPPING

WHERE AND WHEN: *Holly Ridge, Mississippi.*
Late autumn 1929. 'Retta looks out over
Clem Parker's land.

B ELIEVE ME WHEN I TELL YOU THAT BY THE TIME I WAS twelve years old, I had size-nine feet. I was taller than most kids my age, boys even. I had thick hands, and big dreams to be the best I could at every skill and ability I was given. As it turns out, the big dream part started to happen soon after my twelfth birthday. Even though I was still a child, I could pick near to 150 pounds of cotton. That's as much as a full-grown goat weighs.

It's strange how I remember it. I don't recall the picking with my mind. It's my fingertips that hold the memory. My thumbs and pointers and that tall middle finger that stands beside them, and even my pinkies, they're what start to sting whenever I get to recollecting my *pick, pick, picking* frenzy. Both my palms start to burn when I touch back to that high-cotton time. It didn't matter if it was dawn or after sunset, or *can't see* keeping us in the dark. I wasn't working by sight. I was driven by a snowy cotton trance of picking pain.

Blinding white everywhere.

Billowy pillows of little puff-promises. Nettle-headed sprigs and shoots that let me sleep through the dizzy-swirl of a sharecropper's daughter, while at the same time, not once allowing me to rest *my* head on *their* soft heads of hair, as fluffy as my own.

I got to be so good at boxing cotton that the boll weevil came to understand he had no choice but to skip breakfast.

It was around this time when Clem Parker made another promise. He said that if the Little family could pick three hundred pounds more by the season's end, he would pay us a wage that would allow us to save enough to buy our own land. This made Daddy determined. He sang a lot more then. Sang about miracles and joy, and the angel Gabriel's horn, announcing a new day. Sang about the power of having faith.

Daddy hummed and whistled more, too, a tune whose lines I knew. My father rejoiced in the *words* to his faith-hymns, but stuck to the *tune* of a song called "Grinning Fox," not once daring to utter its warning.

Hello, grinning fox.
Who knows, grinning fox?

You say one thing,
but different you do.
Should I put my trust in you?

Your pretty grin
has never told.

That smile, that smile,
could bite my hand,
while being sly.

Or your teeth may drop
a sack of gold.

Who knows, grinning fox?

Who knows?
Who knows?

Seems Daddy was a mix of believing and hesitation. He had two streams of music running in him, clashing tambourines, each seeking to drown out the other.

He was glad to have me back to working all the time. And I was eager to help pick, seeing as it could mean we'd be free of sharecropping's greedy hand, and wouldn't have to portion our crops with anybody.

But I couldn't help but think about Clem's half promises, and the grinning fox.

When I reminded Daddy about Clem being a shiny apple with an uncertain middle, Daddy got quiet, gathered his words carefully.

He said, "You're right, 'Retta, the man can be sometime-y. Sometimes he demeans. Other times he doles out praise and a raise. To that, I will say this. When Clem offers an opportunity that might help our family get ahead, or that could mean a better life for you, I'm willing to take a risk on his whims. It's what I call a father's prerogative."

At night, Daddy had taken to knitting, weaving pearls of sky-bright yarn into snug blue socks. He was a skilled knitter, what some considered women's work. My father believed weaving had nothing to do with *who* did the knitting, just that each stitch be looped and fastened with care.

The leggings he made came up high, to the place just above my knees, where I needed warmth for the colder months, soon to come. My father knitted with gnarled twigs. He stitched with those kindling fingers that would later serve to stoke a fire. Daddy soaked his yarn in goat fat, softening the threads. He called his knitted gift my sapphire socks.

It was an abundant time for our family. The harvest was plentiful that fall. Our crops provided enough squash and collards for sharing at church picnics and prayer meetings.

And goodness, we needed prayer. Knowing we would be able to keep up our end of Clem's arrangement by increasing the pounds of cotton we picked, our family held on to a few kernels of hope.

Clem went back on his promise. He never paid us, not even a cent. It's one thing to give me stale cookies, or to be sometime-y about the way you say a man's name. But it's another to pull the rug out from under a whole family's hopes.

Truth be told, none of us were surprised by Clem's betrayal. But it stung! Made me double-time crabgrass mad! Sent me out to Clem's backyard after dark, when nobody saw. I crouched, yanked out his flowerbeds. Scooped the newly fertilized soil. Gathered its compost, stinking from rotted rinds and cow plop. Heaved—*uuuunngh!*—and flung it at Clem's clean underwear swinging in the nighttime breeze.

Whispered loud inside me, *Wear this smelly mess, Clem, you slippery grinning fox!*

Anybody knows, you need money to buy land, livestock, and horses to start your own farm. We didn't have what it took to get out from Clem's place, so we were forced to stay. Made to live with the humiliation of feeling like we were owned.

I could still pick better than most. But soon winter came. Cotton grew scarce. All our whole family had to go scrapping.

That is low-down work, scrapping. Walking from one plantation to the next, swiping cotton leftovers off the ground, covered with hay shards. It hurt our spirits to be stooping over like that.

One night, warm for December, the moon turned open and showed off its face. Looked to be grimacing, that moon. A mottled ball of butter in a cast-iron sky. Some called it a winter possum moon, since its goldenness invited beady creatures to play under the sky's streaked light. My sisters and I each brought a lantern so we could keep track of one another. Didn't need the lanterns, though. The moon's glow gave off enough.

I heard rustling from the ground's hay-scrap carpet, spread wide. Thought it was possum-play. Took it for critters scurrying among the scraps. But soon into assuming, a quiver-pitched wail flung from the ground's lowest place. Jo-Nelle and Faye were far-off, but they must've heard it, too. I saw their lanterns lift from across the field. Me, being closest to that sharp howl, approached slowly, my lantern low, to not spook the pained creature making its noise. It was a broken wail—*wrrrahhh…wrrr…aahh…wr…wrrrahhh.* There was something measured behind its sound, too. Something deliberate. The cry had certainty in knowing the power of coming on slow.

Only time I'd ever heard a sound like that was when an owl or toad or piglet or possum was cranky and refusing to move. Soon, though, as sudden as that ornery sound began with *wrrrahhh…*, it got quiet and was replaced by rustling.

A night cloud, as white as the cotton-scrap bits under my feet, curled around the moon's edges like a kerchief. This dimmed the sky, making it harder to see near to the ground. I had no choice but to poke my lantern down to cast low light.

No sound came back to greet me. I walked up slow to where the rustling had been. Pushed my lantern's hot hue close to the dry soil, covered with the bed of hay-shards. And what do I see? Two eyes inviting me. Looking straight on, as if they'd been waiting.

I called out, "Jo-Nelle and Faye, come see!"

My sisters got there quick. Our three lanterns brought a tangle of light. Faye was the first to crouch, then me. Jo-Nelle held her lantern steady so's we could all get a good look at what we couldn't believe we were seeing—a half-swaddled baby boy left among the nettles.

Faye lifted the child. The warmth of Jo-Nelle's lantern lit his tiny face, like a brown pie, eyes wide with confusion. He was bigger than an infant, but too small to toddle. For such an itty-bitty baby, he cried some big tears.

Faye placed him at somewhere under one year old. My sister cuddled the boy. She cooed, trying to settle his squirming.

Right off, Faye said, "He's a Night-Deep child."

Jo-Nelle looked pleased, as if we'd happened upon a treasure. "Night-Deep children are deemed lucky."

Faye carefully passed the baby to Jo-Nelle.

"His body is still warm," Jo-Nelle observed. "Means he's only been out here a short time."

My sisters explained that a troubled mother most likely left her young'un behind, not able to care for him in these scrap-gathering days we were all forced to endure. Faye told me that sometimes mothers took a chance leaving their babies to survive in a field, often after misfortune struck, hoping they would become Night-Deep children.

It seemed cruel to abandon a child, but there were mothers whose faith was so strong, trusting their babies could survive, they went ahead with the possibility. Some mothers who didn't have the means to raise their babies claimed to hear the stars speaking, encouraging them to set their infants down under the twinkling sky, confident Providence would arrive.

Anybody who survived a Night-Deep, especially a baby, would become someone who had the power to change bad land to good.

"He's blessed," Faye said.

Jo-Nelle told how the tears of Night-Deep children are believed to trickle into the earth's veins, sending new life to troubled soil.

"Night-Deep young'uns cry more than others," said Jo-Nelle.

"And," Faye described, "when those tears are shed during a Night-Deep, they wash away tribulation, turning sickly soil to healthy, fertile earth. This boy's presence on scrapping land means there's hope on the horizon."

Jo-Nelle said, "Tears flow from Night-Deep babies like rain."

She gently placed the boy in my arms. He was wriggling and wailing.

I adjusted the swaddled cloth that had come loose from around his chin. His head was topped with a cottony cap of dark hair.

Jo-Nelle and Faye lifted their lanterns high, swung them overhead, slicing the night with strokes of light. Their glow-beams sketched circles in the sky.

They chanted a happy affirmation:

Night-Deep child
withstands the dark,
the cursed and brittle land.

You, baby born,
transforming
once-spurned soil,
now blessed with your essence.

Now cleansed with your flowing tears.
Now sacred.
Now bathed.

You, baby born,
wake the night

with high-pitched cries.
Your salty wet washes what's old.
Your salty wet brings new life.

Glories be!

Night-Deep!
Night-Deep!

The baby boy's gaze found its way to my face, rested there, took comfort. Me, I just blinked, whispered, "Who *are* you?"

SLAUGHTERING HOGS

WHERE AND WHEN: *Holly Ridge, Mississippi. Winter 1929. The Little family home, a leaning cabin. 'Retta is perched on the front step.*

W E NAMED THE BABY ROLLINS, MAMA'S SURNAME BEFORE she married Daddy. Called him Roly for short. It was a name that fit him as right as the muslin feed-sack skimmer Jo-Nelle had sewed and now rinsed daily to keep Roly clean. The skimmer tucked perfectly around his chunky thighs and pudgy belly. But it couldn't fully hide Roly's poked-out navel that sat like a twisted clump of dough in the middle of him, where his navel string used to be.

We all took care of Roly, but somehow, I got the job of feeding. Oh, that boy! He was a stubborn bunch of chubby. And greedy about having his way, *the* way he wanted, and when, and how—and now! He ate all the time. But he was particular. He would only eat mashed yams, which were in low supply among our winter food rations.

I tried to feed Roly corn pone or turnip broth. He was not having it. And coaxing did not work on this boy. With Roly, wheedling was a waste of time. Trying to persuade him did the opposite. It made Roly dig his baby heels deeper into the dirt of his own obstinate ways of behaving.

Roly was the slowest eater ever, too. I often wondered why fate put this boy with us. Particular and dawdling were not ways to be with my people, especially when it came to food.

We were grateful for whatever sustenance we had, and pleased in the partaking.

To help provide for all of us, Faye and Jo-Nelle took to slaughtering hogs for plantation owners who lived nearby. The farmers didn't pay them with money. What they gave in exchange for my sisters' work was worse than piddly wages, and it smelled. They threw scraps that Jo-Nelle and Faye had little choice but to take. My proud, beautiful sisters accepted pigs' feet and hog intestines for their services. While they worked, I worked, too—tending to Roly, who was now fully sitting up and always *spitting* up, and refusing everything, and whining and moaning while his baby teeth cut through tender gums. I had to rinse his cotton skimmer whenever its pee smell settled too strongly, and especially when mud-poop leaked from his rag-diaper. I will be very honest in admitting that sometimes I let the mud-poop crust over and the pee-stink dry before changing Roly. His defiance seemed to be rubbing off on me. There were times when I just *did not want to.*

Boxing cotton was easier than minding Roly. Boll weevils were only half as dogged as this little child with meaty fists like baby hams. I tried rubbing his sore gums with my pointer finger, first dipping it in sugar water to sweeten my skin. But

Roly, could he ever bite! Once, his tiny ragged teeth even drew blood from my thick-skinned hands.

I snapped, "Boy-child, you are a prickly thistle!"

When Roly got to wailing, he was hard-pressed to stop. I sang the Night-Deep chant, which never worked to soothe him.

Then I found a way to calm him down with a game I came to call *Peek-a-you—blue!*

I teased Roly's eyes by dangling my sapphire socks, tickling his lids and cheeks and chin, letting the soft blue toes bring a giggle to both of us.

Peek-a-who?
Peek-a-YOU!
Soft-soft sky.
Oh, so blue!

Daddy's sapphire sock magic was one of the good things about tending to Roly. The other was that I didn't have to slaughter hogs. Somehow Jo-Nelle and Faye could always find the good in the ugly, though. Even in swine hooves. They chopped and diced those fatty pig parts. Mixed them with onions. Made thick stews for winter nights. And somewhere along the way, Roly started to enjoy the stews, too.

But Daddy, he had lost sight of any good. As winter's pale sky grew colder, he stopped singing.

My father.

Silent.

Sullen.

Sinking.

BUG SPRAY

WHEN AND WHERE: *From the days of sharecropping labor to the present, throughout many American states. A US map projects on a screen, dotted with decals that pinpoint the regions where sharecropping was prevalent. Mississippi. Louisiana. Florida. Alabama. Georgia. 'Retta is restless. She's speaking on behalf of many sufferers.*

WORD WAS, FARMERS WERE TRYING SOMETHING NEW TO control their boll weevils and other bugs. First time it came, we stopped what we were doing, winced at the mist blurring the horizon, and watched to see what this strange thing would do.

We couldn't duck, hide, escape, or run.

We had to keep working while the machine on wheels with the spider legs sent the contraption's command:

Ready, aim—spray!

As we crouched and picked and reached, we couldn't help but hold every bit of our breath, shut our eyes tight, and pray the pesticides would be kind.

We never knew when the spray would come.

This was what they were calling a test.

An *experiment.*

A *try-and-see.*

On the days when it came, down on our knees we prayed the stinging spray wouldn't fill our lungs. That juice was meant to kill the bugs and slugs who lived on leaves and burrowed among the vines, feasting on lettuce heads and tobacco.

Whenever the *try-and-see* reared up, I covered my whole face with both hands, waited, fixed my mind on the sky's clouds, far away from the spray.

Up there, I *could* escape.

Up there, my mind was high above the *try-and-see*.

But still, it made us cough. Struggle. Scatter. We worked hard not to inhale as we waited for *ready, aim, spray* to go away.

Until tomorrow.

Ever since that day, I held the same beliefs about that bug spray. As much as I bemoaned boll weevils, the truth is, none of nature's creatures deserves a death sent like a rain shower that settles softly and smothers us whole.

Over time, *try-and-see* became *more-and-more*. The memory of it still burns. We didn't know it then, but that rain was poison scouring our skin.

When its rolling hose spit that silver mist, it was trying with a will to rinse us clean of our dignity.

PEOPLE ALL SAYING

WHERE AND WHEN: *Holly Ridge, Mississippi.*
March 1930. 'Retta tucks her head,
pulls into herself.

ADN'T HEARD DADDY SING IN MONTHS, AND SOON I knew why. Daddy got cancer in his lungs and throat. At church I heard the whispers of people all saying it was from the bug spray.

My daddy couldn't work. Couldn't speak. His singing was a memory. That was the sharpest cut of all. Being so weak, Daddy struggled to hug me. But by then, I'd grown even stronger.

I could hug *him* plenty.

Me and my sisters, we took turns helping to feed Daddy, who had become feeble. Even in his weakness, Daddy always summoned enough strength to give his 'Retta a tiny smile. A time or two, he even held baby Roly, who was as big and as weighty as a flour-filled feed-sack. It was mostly me doing the hoisting and holding, supporting Roly's heft and Daddy's rail-thin wrists with both my arms.

In time, Daddy's little bit of happy-to-see-me ended. The lids of my father's eyes turned to heavy hoods. His breathing became a rattly mess of sound. Cancer growled and snarled like an angry wolf.

Then one evening, nighttime's dark cape rushed in to show us the Big Dipper's bounty. I have never witnessed stars so bright as on that night. *Can't see* sprinkled heaven's glitter above us.

Those hooded lids on my father's eyes curled themselves over his half gaze. The tired wheeze that was keeping Daddy alive slipped away, and he died.

GLISTENING HINGES

WHERE AND WHEN: *Holly Ridge, Mississippi.*
Days later. Darkness. Blue light from above.
'Retta holds a candle. Its tiny flame sends
warm glints to her chin and cheeks.

F YOU'VE EVER HAD TO PLUNGE YOUR FACE INTO A MUDDY swamp to search for a crawfish or crabs, holding your breath and your heart at the same time, praying you'll make it until you get to where good air lets you gulp, and where dirt-water stops pressing and settling into every crack of you—that's what it's like to watch your father slip away to an unknown place.

With Daddy gone, I woke many nights, startled from bad dreams, not able to sleep, weeping. Cried like baby Roly did in that dark field, wanting comfort, groaning from a deep place. From the swamp of my insides with no bottom to its grief.

Huh-gggrree...eeeee...heh...heh...unh...unh...whuh...

On one of those nights when wailing came on like a hard storm, I saw a bright vision. Reached for it in my half dream, until it came on pure, pushing beyond blackness.

Saw it all, real clear.

There they were.

Together, finally.

Delia, my mother, and Gideon, Daddy, sitting pretty in what we call our Golden Angel Cypress. A sprawling elder tree, one of the oldest in these parts, the hearsay being that its branches hold the souls of folks passed-on.

Dressed in crisp white, each of them.

46

Mama, wearing a silk-and-lace dress, like for a wedding.

Daddy's suit, so dignified. Pride, the whole way about him.

Golden branches reached to heaven's front porch, always open, welcoming these two who've been called Home.

If you climbed the porch steps, to a door, its glistening hinges whispering the rhythms of angel-music.

No squeaking here. No rust, neither.

Here was filled with easy, bountiful, smooth, and free.

Amazing grace, how sweet the sound.

This was the place only high-up clouds can touch.

Here the Big Dipper spills honeyed tea.

It was still hard to sleep most nights. Come many mornings, I woke with a tearstained face. But the glistening hinges gave me a bright place to look.

After that, when life's rust came, when everything seemed to squeak, I fixed my eyes on that Golden Angel Cypress tree.

I set my gaze toward that glistening door, on Home, high-up.

Because, knowing that Daddy and Mama were together again, dancing to angel-rhythms, lifted the sadness that churned in all my whole heart.

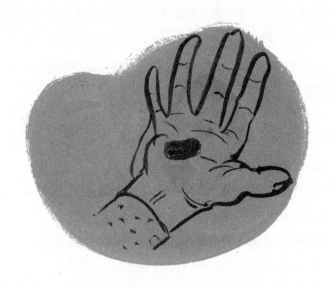

THE M-AND-THE-S

WHERE AND WHEN: *Holly Ridge, Mississippi.*
Summer 1930. Beneath a large shade tree that stands at
the edge of a dusty path leading to the entrance of the
Parker land. 'Retta has a slight limp. She makes her way
to a tree-swing. Steadies herself for support. Slides onto
the swing's flat wooden seat. Rocks slowly.

WAS NEAR TO THIRTEEN WHEN THE DOCTOR TOLD ME I HAD the sickness. First thing I asked him was how somebody like me, strong as a tree, can get something that makes a person so weak.

Had bug spray's poison rained down on me?

Had Daddy's cancer somehow found its way to his 'Retta?

Doctor told me this didn't have nothing to do with being strong, or with any kind of spray. Said what I have is a disease that happens in the nerves, and that it's not from anything I did, or got sprayed around me. Said it just comes on in some people, even a hearty girl.

Well, maybe so, but numb fingers, headaches, a tight back, and tired limbs that flare up every so now and again are no fun for *this* girl.

We were still working on Clem Parker's land at that time. It was Clem's idea to have the county doctor take a look at me. He sure didn't want his best picker getting sick. This had nothing to do with Clem caring whether I was feeling well or not. My quick picking was like a honed tool. Clem wanted to make sure I was working as best I could.

When I didn't make it to the fields for two days straight, on account of my legs being stiff, and numbness rising in me, and my head feeling like it had been filled with a bag of heavy stones, Clem sent for the man with a medical bag. The doctor came to the house, all serious. I recognized him from once when Clem had him come check on Daddy. Back then, I hadn't got an up-close look. Only saw the man with his black satchel come and go from way off.

I didn't trust the doctor at first. Faye and Jo-Nelle didn't, neither. From when Daddy was sick, and even before that, I'd been warned about White doctors treating Colored patients. Been told not to trust them, not even a little. People all saying if you're Colored, don't ever mouth-off or disagree with a White doctor, else he might give you what's called *the black pill*.

That was what folks claimed. The hearsay was that the black pill was filled with a strange kind of medicine White doctors slipped to Colored people who, once they'd swallowed the pill, were never heard from again. The scuttlebutt said things like, "Didn't you know? Willie Sims, he got a cough. Doctor took one look at him, gave Willie the black pill, and—*thud!*—Willie reeled back, fell flat, and that was the end of him."

Right off, I noticed two things about Clem's doctor. Peculiar things. The first was the skin on his hands. It was like the skin on the underside of a baby pig. Soft and pink, and smooth. How could a grown-man doctor have hands like that? He had never touched a prickly thistle, that's for sure. But those hands made me wonder, *Hadn't he ever put stitches in a split lip, or set broken bones, or brought babies into this world?* There was no wear or tear on his hands to prove he'd done any healing.

The second strange thing I noticed had to do with the doctor's eyes. They were toady colored. Part green, part brown, with flecks of gold that glistened, even when he shaded his eyes from the sunlight's glare. More than that, though, I had never seen an expression in the eyes of a White man that was anything similar to this doctor's.

I couldn't name his expression, first off. But when the doctor put his pig-soft palms to each side of my neck, he was so gentle. And, just as strange, when he met me with his gaze, I saw caring in his toady eyes.

There was another thing, too. It was startling. Here was a White man looking *at* me, straight on. He wasn't casting his eyes above mine, or shifting them left and right, or to the sky, or to something else to avoid ever having to look at me.

I wanted to ask him if he had even gone to doctor school, and if he did, did he read the doctor-school books, and did he understand what they said. Because if he could read good enough to learn about medicine, then he could also understand that this was Mississippi, and that on the whole, White people didn't bother to look at Colored people in their eyes, let alone help them when they were sick.

Something in me liked this doctor, but something else in me, deep down, refused to trust him fully. I pressed my lips tightly closed, for fear that he might try to slip me the black pill. The toady-eyed doctor asked me to stick out my tongue, but you can best believe I was not going to give him a way to get that pill in! I kept my lips as tight as the lid on a pickle jar. Shook my head. I would not be saying *ahhh* for him.

Whatever the doctor told me about any ailments I might have, I didn't let myself believe him. I could have been suffering from a bad case of gout or a hammertoe, and this man would be up in my face telling me, strong as a tree, that I got something deadly. No, no. Not me. Maybe when the doctor was in doctor school, that was the medical lesson he missed. Maybe *he'd* been out sick on that day in doctor college.

After the doctor examined me—felt at my knees and shins and elbows and back, listened to my heart with his cold coin on a cord—he spoke to Jo-Nelle and Faye, apart from me. Then, on the path leading to the main road, the doctor had a conversation with Clem.

My sisters came to me right after. Told me I'd been stricken with what the doctor said was called multiple sclerosis. The doctor explained to Faye and Jo-Nelle that soon I would be too weak and too slow to spend long days picking cotton.

My sisters told me the disease probably wasn't bad enough to fully sacrifice my limbs, but only time would tell. Thankfully, I could still walk and talk and mostly be me, but slower, and not as strong as a tree.

But that condition, it did knock the wind out of me on occasion. Weakened my legs, took away my nimble. Cut me down to half speed. I decided I would call the disease the M-and-the-S for short, on account of who had time to be saying that long name with all those l's and syllables that could get twisted up on my tongue.

Knowing their baby sister would now be living with the M-and-the-S made Jo-Nelle and Faye sad, and it made Clem Parker all kinds of mad. He was about to lose his prize picker. Most of all, this M-and-S mess made me wonder, *Why me, 'Retta Little, strong as a tree?*

And even though the doctor had told me that bug spray had nothing to do with it, I couldn't help but wonder, too, if that was true.

I made a choice then. Though the doctor said I *had* the M-and-the-S, I would not allow the M-and-the-S to *have* me. And besides, M-and-S could stand for different things, depending on how you looked at those letters.

M-and-S could mean Meek-and-Small or Mighty-and-Strong.

Figured it this way. I came to this world with twos of plenty of things. And was blessed with ones on plenty of others. I've got two legs. Two arms. Along with them, I've been given a one-and-only mouth. It was time to appreciate my two arms and legs for everything they could do for me, and to put my one-and-only mouth to some Mighty-and-Strong use. In time, this would happen in ways I never could've expected.

Meanwhile, the only ones happy about my weakened limbs were the boll weevils, who didn't seem to even blink at the bug spray. They were as alive as ever, and still ready to chomp at the slow-to-go cotton that would be waiting for them to enjoy, because pick-it-fast 'Retta Little would not be in the fields at *can't see* depriving them of their morning meal.

MARBLES

WHERE AND WHEN: *Holly Ridge, Mississippi.
Fall 1930. 'Retta rakes leaves that have collected at the
base of Clem Parker's shade tree. It is the same towering
oak that holds a tree-swing, and that stands watch at
the edge of the plantation entry road.*

THE GIRL WITH THE BUTTERFLY HAND WAS AS UNEXPECTED as snow flurries in July.

When the doctor came back to Clem Parker's farm, he had a child with him. A girl who looked to be my same age. This time, the doctor was there to see somebody other than me. All right, because I was not in the mood for more bad news about how rickety I'd be walking, come years from now. It was someone else's turn to put a button on both lips so the black pill could not be slipped in.

When the doctor got out of his big black car to find the poor soul he'd be examining on that day, he told the girl to stay put.

I could see right off she was not about keeping still or staying. She sat at the up-front of the doctor's vehicle, playing with the steering wheel, making faces like she was driving fast in some kind of crazy race. It wasn't long before she got sick of that game, came out of the car, and sat herself on a patch of dry dirt by the hind fender.

They say when you see somebody disobeying to ignore it. But when that girl waved me over, how could I pretend to not see? I tried to keep my eyes on my rake. She wouldn't give up, though. The girl just kept waving me to come closer. When she saw that I was working hard to shrug her off, she held up a calico pouch. Started shaking it. Clatter sounds shot out from the bag. The clinking was quiet at first, but then grew louder and more rattly as she shook the sack in one hand and summoned me with the other.

Well, dang. I had to at least tell her to stop making noise.

And that she was misbehaving.

And that she was going against what the doctor said for her to do.

And that she'd best get back into the car like she was told.

I set down my rake, walked up to her. This is why minding your own business is always a good idea.

Before I could even start in on what-all I was ready to say, she asked me if I knew anything about playing marbles. But I was not there to play. I needed to be working.

When I shook my head no, to mean I should not be standing there talking to a stranger, she took it to signify that I didn't know how to play marbles. That was the truth. I had never even seen a marble, let alone played with one. But this girl was seven steps ahead of me before I could even speak.

She was quick to spill the bunch of tiny glass balls onto the dirt. With her finger, she scratched a firm circle around the balls to close them in. Told me these were her special marbles, and let's play.

The girl's hair was a wheat-sheath cap, held away from her face by two bobby pins. Her fingernails had been bitten down to patches.

It was then that I noticed the beet-colored blotch on the top of her hand. Looked like a butterfly, eager to lift itself off her skin, in a hurry to flutter away.

She saw me looking. Told me what seemed like something she'd been explaining her whole life.

"Was born with the mark. My daddy, he says it's good luck and the reason I win at anything I put my hands to, including marbles."

I nodded.

"My name's Toby, a boy's name, because I'm really named Tabitha, but don't like it, so I tell everybody to call me Toby, and that's that. And all right, then."

Whew, could Toby ever talk! She had a motor on her tongue, and it just kept running.

"I'm the doctor's daughter, and I can teach you to play marbles, and what's your name? And I like your rake."

"'Retta," was the only thing I could get to come out of my mouth. And somehow I was now sitting cross-legged on the ground next to Toby, sizing up the marbles inside the circle she'd drawn on the dirt.

There were two marbles bigger than the others.

"The shooter marbles," Toby told me.

She gave each of us one of those little swirled-glass balls. Hers was a shock of green. A bundle of clovers rolled into a bright nugget. Toby was eager to let me know her shooter was a special marble called an emerald agate.

My shooter was as yellow as an egg yolk, and an agate, too. An *amarillo agate*, she said was the proper name.

The amarillo agate caught the afternoon's sun. The marble's shimmer put fiddle music inside my mind. It had a firelight like I had never seen before or after, ever.

Toby showed me how to use the shooter to flick the other marbles out of the circle. We took turns. Her first.

She was not kidding when she said her butterfly hand was lucky. Toby could knock two marbles out of the circle at the same time by fast-flinging her emerald agate with her thumb's knuckle.

She liked to tell me that, too, praising herself like she'd stepped back to watch her own game.

"Yeah, yeah, yeah—Toby's got quick-flick fingers!" she called out.

Me, well, I was wishing for a butterfly hand of my own. My egg-yolk marble had a miserable spin on it. The only thing

I knocked out from the circle in the dirt was more dirt. But watching Toby and the gleam of the amarillo agate turned the fiddle music in my mind into an all-out band of stomping jig-time fun.

Well, too much of what I was not supposed to be doing came to a fast stop when I heard Jo-Nelle calling out for me. Her hollering was like being shook from a happy dream, and being forced to come to your senses about what's truly real.

You have never seen me grab back a rake so fast. 'Cause here come Jo-Nelle looking for me. She was far off near the house, her shape a tiny might on the horizon. But even so, my sister had a cowbell of a mouth.

"'Retta!"

Soon as she spotted me, she turned back, didn't bother to come closer for scolding me.

Not far behind was the doctor, calling for Toby. I guess he could see that his daughter was no longer in the front seat of their car.

Before the doctor's girl with the butterfly hand scooped up her marbles, she uncurled my fingers from the rake's long wooden handle.

"When you're not raking, 'Retta, you can keep your hands busy with *this*."

Toby pressed the yolk-colored shooter firm into my palm, then fixed herself to behind the steering wheel of her daddy's big black automobile.

I slipped the golden marble into my pocket. It was warm against my leg. That fiddle music seemed to play from inside the fabric folds of my apron. This made pushing the leaves with my rake's teeth much easier.

As the doctor drove off, Toby and me, we waved and waved.

Later, I tucked that sun-colored marble into one of the heels of my sapphire socks that had been drying on a clothesline. Kept the agate snug by knotting the sock's ankle so's to make a pouch. I swear that marble glowed. Its bright eye glistened, sending glints through the soft blue, lighting my sock from the inside out.

TREES

WHERE AND WHEN: *Holly Ridge, Mississippi.*
Late autumn 1930. Tall oaks create a canopy, enclosing
'Retta. She takes in the trees' beauty, delighting in
their massive splendor.

ABY ROLY HAD HIS EYES WIDE OPEN TO EVERYTHING, ALL the time.

When he saw something move—firefly, horsetail, tree leaf—right away, he grabbed at it.

Soon Roly was starting to walk. He toddled slowly, but always in a sure direction, as if he was going someplace important.

To keep his balance, Roly moved with both arms out front.

I teased that boy, "Here you are, pronouncing good news."

Roly loved the shade of this land's tallest oaks. I will always remember the day Roly's first words came. It was the roots, trunks, bark, and branches that brought him to talking. What he said tumbled from his pudgy lips, wet with drool. It was a baby's proclamation. Roly let loose his decree, reached for the high-up, outstretched limbs of a cinnamon oak, now barren, its leaves rustling under Roly's feet.

Roly's speaking called the birds with what sounded like a song, inviting all to join in.

"Me...a...treeeee!"

There was a happy skip-step to Roly's toddling.

With arms up and out, and rejoicing, Roly motioned me to dance with him at this little party.

I was happy to oblige. Stretched my arms high to the sky, following Roly's lead.

"*Me...a...treeeee!*" Roly sang.

I knelt to meet Roly, nose-to-nose. Joined him, singing.

"*We...a...treeeee!*"

"*Us...free!*"

ROLY
1942 to 1950

SLOW SUNRISE

Daybreak's tawny fingers climb the horizon,
baking the edges of unfurling fields.
The land is alive with color.

Cuke-blankets.
Strawberry snatches, bright, sweet.
Ruffle-topped lettuce heads.
Carrots crops — rooted.

These, Nature's gifts,
are all brought to barren land
by the hand of a farmer, also gifted.

Who is that planter, standing firm,
bathed in slow-growing ochre splashes
that wash his stocky frame like warm rain?

As he enters, Loretta,
a guiding presence,

hushed in the background,
watches on.

Her brother,
no longer a crybaby.

Now, he's got a mind of his own,
and some big opinions to fill it.

Colors as bright as Magnolia's white-flag petals,
flap in heated winds.

The music of a drowsy horn rises.
Puts a stomp-rhythm to his walk.

His voice, low and steady,
begins a blues tune,
crooning and crying out
against what feels like a heel
tamping down on the truth about troubled waters.

The music fades.

In one hand, he's holding a newspaper,
filled with stories that are signs of times.

In another, he grips his trusted friend:
The Old Farmer's Almanac.

Holding,
  he's always holding on.
Holding
  his head high.
Holding
  his breath.
Hoping
  those signs of the times will change,
  between the between.

Slowly, silently, he makes his way.
To say what he knows we need to hear.
Comes right up to the edge of our understanding.

Morning's mist has turned to a new hue,
marking the start of his story.

It begins with day-clean's glimmer,
then turns to Red Raw Rage, tucked deep.
Lit from behind.
Burning from inside.

Who are you, gifted farmer?

Like those fruits and vegetables that rise from dust-soil,
he needs time to grow.
Slow, steady. That's his way.

He introduces who he is,
by first letting go his held breath.
Turns his eyes to what he does best —
working the land and rejoicing in the creatures
that cakewalk in their pen.

Well, uh-huh, then.

Starts in again with his easy tune. The reds turn cool.
Roly, now grown, brings us back to when he was a boy.

Speaks his blues.

W ELL, *UH-HUH*, THEN, I WAS FOUND IN A BED OF HAY, BUT I ain't no kind of needle. Needles, they's skinny, prickly, and mean. That ain't me. No, I'm what they call a Night-Deep child. Came into this world with a special connection to the earth's abundance and its creatures.

Me, I gots a gift for daffodils, bee-keeping, and pole beans. Born with a steady hand at making something beautiful grow from brittle soil. Don't know *how* I do it. Just *that* I do. Bringing crops alive. Comes natural. Something sweet from something shriveled. I'm also blessed with the ability to monitor time, read, and roll pie crusts. Give me a clock and a recipe, and I will make good happen.

And animals, when we're together, we bring rhythms.

Since from when 'Retta and I was kids, she has always accused me of being mule-headed. Saying it's *my* way or no way. Saying I been like that from always.

Still stubborn, she say.

But let me tell you my side of why I'm in no hurry. And my reasons for standing firm in what I believe's right. Started from during my boyhood. I gots a special way when it comes to understanding what keeps this world's miracles on course, on their seasons.

So, go 'head. Call me mule-headed. I *am* smart about mules. And geese. And cows. And our sow.

Truth is, I know 'bout lots of things.

Reaching is one of them. I'm certain 'bout reaching. Sure of it.

When suffering runs up from behind, you reach for whatever grit you gots inside.

When hatred follows you home, you reach for the darkest hiding place you can find, 'specially in deepest night.

When the moon winks, you meet it by reaching with your eyes. By keeping the sky's glowing hope inside you, where you reach for that, too.

Now, here's what I *don't* know.

Don't know why my ma and pa left me on the hay-scrap of an open field.

Don't know when my true birthday is.

Don't know if I will ever be the same after that evil day, guessing to be when I was eleven, nearing twelve years old.

Well, *uh-huh*, then, I'm gon' reach back, and tell how it all went.

I'm gon' speak on it. *My* way.

CLOCK-KEEPER

WHERE AND WHEN: *Ruleville, Mississippi. Spring 1942.*
The Nate Gaston plantation. Roly leans on the fence
that divides the Little land from the Gaston property.

THEM THAT RAISED ME, MY SISTERS, 'RETTA, JO-NELLE, and Faye, they was able to buy our own plot of land from a man named Nate Gaston. Faye and Jo-Nelle had saved every penny they earned from scrapping. They took on all kinds of work to make money. Did laundry, mended plantation owners' clothes, made pine soap to bring in cash, until, after years of scrimping, they'd saved enough to purchase property with our family's name on the deed.

Lived not far from Clem Parker's. The place was a snatch of soil and trees. To us, it was a big wish come true. We bought goats and mules. And chickens and cows that was ours only. This was the Littles', make no mistake. To keep what was now rightly ours, though, we still had to work for Nate Gaston on his property.

He, that man, made us call him *Sir-Sir.*

Now what kind of name is that?

Sir-Sir.

Hisses like an achy snake.

Sirrrr-sirrrr.

Well *uh-huh,* anyway, that was the name Nate Gaston wanted. Seeing as Sir-Sir was the boss of us, we obliged that snake-name.

Sir-Sir's farm was the same as Parker's. Swarming with Colored folk hunched over in dusty fields, dry as our dreams for anything better. I worked 'longside my sisters. We all picked, chopped, hauled, and hacked, putting our sweat into being sharecroppers. Even though what was ours was ours, and even though my sisters could earn small bits of extra money doing other kinds of work, for the most part, we still depended on Sir-Sir for our livelihood. Same tired thing as all the other sharecropping set-ups. We earned very little money, which kept us tied to Sir-Sir's rope.

I was determined to keep reaching for something better. Through their example, my sisters let me see there was always work to be done for earning extra money. I polished Sir-Sir's floors. Washed, hung, and folded his drawers. My sisters taught me to bake pies. Maple-peach splitting open, oozing thick in the middle, was a special sweet I learned to make on my own. Them pies brought in twenty-five whole cents each!

I fed and bathed Sir-Sir's dogs, too, and did whatever else Missus Gaston—who, behind her back, we all called Missus Sir-Sir, same like her husband—asked me to. And let me tell you, that woman was a mix between a heap of nervous hens and a hound. Her feathers stayed puffed. And, *uh-huh*, could she ever howl.

I started to think Missus Sir-Sir liked yapping my name, just to be yapping my name.

Roly, do this! Roly, do that! Roly—do, do, do!

That yap-noise would've stepped on lots of people's belief in themselves, but it made me stronger somehow. When, firstly, I started in with working for Missus Sir-Sir, it bothered her that I don't move fast. I do what needs doing with steady steps.

My pace had a good result with Missus Sir-Sir. In time, she stopped yapping. *Do, do, do* changed course like a wild storm-wind, and moved to simple acceptance of my ways. Missus Sir-Sir came to see that I *do* do, *how* I do, and that it all gits done. She even took to thanking me for my chores. The maple-peach pies I baked for the Gaston family also helped calm down that jittery woman.

Her husband, Sir-Sir, he was another story. He could be mean, but he wasn't stupid. When he come to find out how good I could read, write, and figure, he saw dollar signs. Took me off-a field-work and put me on as his clock-keeper, thinking I could somehow make the work go faster by watching the time.

People say to don't let a White person know how truly smart you are, else they'll take it out badly on you.

But that's negativity at work, making you believe *not* to

believe in your own abilities. Since I do *how* I do, I was not going to hide none of it.

Sir-Sir wanted that everything be done in half the time. But rushing is a waste. It brings mistakes. Forces you to repeat, *re*do, or start over.

I put my best into being Sir-Sir's timekeeper. Made sure everything happened exactly when it was supposed to. Not a minute before, and for certain not a minute afterward. I was mindful. There was no mistaking me being punctual about work schedules and delivery times, at the exact moments they were meant to happen.

Once, when Sir-Sir was irritable, and pressing me to hurry for no reason, I found myself sassing him.

Told Sir-Sir to slow hisself down. To don't give up five minutes 'fore a miracle happens. And on God's watch, five minutes might mean five days, fifty months, or five-times-five years. Told him trusting in Nature's clock is what it means to have faith, even when it's slower than he'd like.

Wish I'd bit down on my tongue.

Why didn't I think before speaking?

'Cause even though I do *how* I do, I will always wonder if what came to pass after that was somehow the *doing* of my sass-words to Sir-Sir.

CAKEWALK

WHERE AND WHEN: *Ruleville, Mississippi.*
June 1942. The Little scab of land tucked behind
the main parcel that belongs to Nate Gaston. Roly is
throwing feed, calling the animals to eat.
Morning rises.

S OON AS CAKEWALK BROKE OPEN HIS SHELL, I KNEW HE was not like any other gosling. He didn't just hatch from an egg. No, no. That feisty bird peck-pecked, shimmied, and danced the wet from his newborn feathers. Naming him was easy. He took pride in what it meant to strut.

The baby bird greeted me every day at dawn when I rustled the grain in my feed bucket that signaled the start of Cakewalk's play.

"Bird, *come!*" I called. "Do your dance!"

Sure enough, he quick-stepped.

Honked.

Waddled to where I was.

Pecked my chin with his eager beak.

Waited.

Sauntered in a circle, twice, then again.

Took a second pause.

Looped back.

Crisscrossed the yard.

Swiveled his neck.

Let his feet talk.

"Cakewalk, you gots a bird-rhythm gift!"

He liked when I said that. Always answered back.

Gwank! Gwank! The sound of baying hounds, mixed with throat squeaks. *Gwank! Gwank!*

My feisty gosling celebrated each new day while the other animals gathered to watch. They were an audience of feathers, manes, hooves, snouts, and tails. There were udders, too, and plenty to *moo* and *meow* about.

It was me who'd named the animals in our pen.

Our mule—*Ash*, on account of his color.

Whenever I spoke to him, I punched the air. Marched, too.

Turned my mule's name into a loud parade.

"Ash, brash! Brash Ash!"

This made his ears wiggle.

Our sow, I named *Q*, 'cause of how her tail, high on her rump, curled and poked out at its bottom.

The best way to see a sow smile is to tell her she's royal. So every chance I could, I told her, "Big pig, you're a queen!"

Soon as I said *queen*, my pig's lips turned up, happy.

Our tabby barn cat, her name was *Stray*, since she showed up one day, moved in, birthed kittens, and stayed.

"You's a fuzzy-fir kitty," was how I talked to our cat. That made her whiskers twitch.

Our cow, I named her *Patch*, from the pretty mix of black and white that decorated her coat.

"Patch, you's the best-dressed beast in Ruleville."

Whenever I proclaimed this, Patch affirmed it by tail-swatting flies from her backside.

Cakewalk's ma, I'd named her *Swank*, being a goose with an attitude.

We could sure have us some fun, shimmying together, Swank and me.

Every day, I told her, "Goose, work your caboose!"

There was no mistaking Cakewalk belonged to Swank. Like his ma, he was smart. He knew I mixed love into his food. I scattered the grain with a sure rhythm. Cakewalk's sister goslings squabbled over their feed. But not Cakewalk. Time and again, I praised him for having manners.

"Bird, you ain't no kind of squabbler."

When all the kernels were out from my feed bucket, I settled in the center of the pen, sat and waited for what I knew was coming next.

"Lay it *on* me, bird!"

Before even partaking of the corn-seed mix, Cakewalk peck-pecked my chin again, and once more after. He settled in my lap, nibbled the grain from both my hands.

"Cakewalk," I said, "you're my good-bird friend."

RAIN

WHERE AND WHEN: *Ruleville, Mississippi.*
July 4, 1942. Roly is perched on a tree stump, feet
dangling. He's shucking ears of corn, carefully removing
their husk strands. Rocks while he talks.

'RETTA, BEING GROWED UP NOW, YOU'D THINK SHE AND I were done with quarreling. But *uh-huh*, sometimes we could go heavy with disagreements, arguing about everything from weather patterns to horse habits. Today, we debated 'bout rain.

It was Independence Day. I was braiding corn-husk tassels for waving and celebrating.

'Retta put that book under my nose, tapped her finger on the page showing 'bout today. She said, "The almanac predicts rain."

Told my sister, "No, that ain't right. Even the almanac makes mistakes."

"Not hardly," 'Retta insisted. "There's a storm smell in the air."

"Smells can fool you," I said back quick.

I was convinced there was little chance we'd see rain today, and 'specially not a storm. The animals were out, enjoying the afternoon's clear sky. Not even a puff-cloud dotted the blue.

If a storm *was* on its way, Cakewalk, he would've fled after his morning dance. Our barn cats, they'da for sure be hiding between fence beams. Cows and calves huddle when a storm's brewin'. Today, Patch and her young'uns were as lazy and as happy as ever.

'Retta closed the book, tucked it at her elbow.

"Suit yourself, know-it-all boy."

I slapped her forehead with my husk tassels, pretending to make it hurt. My now-growed sister stuck out her tongue, left me there smirking.

I was right 'bout the rain. Besides, in Mississippi on the Fourth of July, storms do *not* happen. It's so hot, even peaches pray for rain that don't come.

So, boo to any smells playing nose-tricks on this day of tassels and pie.

That's the best part 'bout July Fourth. Fruits are ready for the occasion. Red and blue grapes split-open, seep their sweet juices.

When I shut my eyes and pucker, I can taste the skin surrounding the sweetness of them berries and grapes. Little fruit-jewels. I can feel the slippery joy of them grapes as I suck on their cotton-candy sugar-goodness.

Every grape holds a special secret. A burst of flavor that pockets its seeds.

Uh-huh, them seeds. Them little pits inside a grape's soul.

So many folks spit their seeds. Fling them from the tips of their tongues. But I ain't quick to spit.

Seeds are tiny treasures.

Seeds hold the secrets of tomorrow.

Seeds spread the future of beautiful fruit that can shoot and prosper, once pressed down in the earth.

When seeds are nurtured, they grow into gifts.

It's that simple.

We are seeds, if we choose to be. I wish I'da had the wherewithal to tell that to 'Retta. Well, it was not too late to share the gifts of this day. I knelt in the side yard, started picking the vine grapes in their bunches, collecting them in the grain bucket I'd rested on the fence post after feeding the animals.

Anybody knows you can't pick grapes without sampling. It's rude to refuse Nature's generosity. And so, for manners' sake, I could not help but partake in the grapes.

Soon into the picking and slurping, a strange swirl of circumstances swept in. None of them had anything to do with the other. There was no sense to it, no reasonable reason.

Suddenly, all at once, the world turned upside down.

The warm juice from them grapes started to mess with my insides, churning and hurting. The agitation seemed to call in a veil of fog. Twisting clouds wound their way forward. Mop-water filled the sky, roiling, same as what was going on inside my belly. Then came an odor. Stunk like rotten eggs mixed with decaying yolks.

From across the silence of this peaceful afternoon, a sharp sound crackled. Rumbles rose up. The horizon turned the color of mustard. Thunder flung through the whole yard. Blue lightning, too.

Our animals scattered, whined, hid.

A sway of wind turned to sudden, drenching rains.

Hail came, hurling ice teeth on this July day!

The grapes in my belly would not stay down. They escaped my stomach.

I crouched, begged—surrendered to the grape gravy hurling up and out. The feed bucket slid out from my fingers. As I managed to make my way to our cabin, a moan swelled from someplace deep. That low sound snarled a warning from my insides.

These peculiar happenings could only mean one thing.

Omen!

HARDSHIP'S FIST

WHERE AND WHEN: *Ruleville, Mississippi. Autumn 1942. Dawn has sliced open the sky's amber tint. Roly stands in front of his barn's newly painted slats. The planks bring a glistening crimson backdrop to his indigo overalls. These hues of morning's expectation, soon betrayed.*

TRIED WITH A WILL TO CHASE AWAY THAT SUMMER DAY memory. But it hung on, stuck to me like bugs on fly-paper.

Soon after our family got a few kernels of happiness from owning land and animals, hardship's fist came down.

It was the height of our harvest season, bringing abundant crops, everything blooming, boasting its bounty.

Tomatoes, fat, fleshy. Parsnips, thick. Melons, proud.

October rolled in. This day's morning brought a warm mist blanket, peeling off night, welcoming dawn.

Like always, I woke early to feed our animals. Didn't take me but a moment to know there'd been trouble. Sensed mis-doing, soon as I approached the henhouse. Smelled the beginnings of putrid. Same odor as on that strange hailstorm day, back in July.

But this time, it wasn't my nose that picked up the strange smell. The stink was stronger than that. It was a queasy greeting, way far down in my belly's belly. It churned like with those grapes. But ever since that summer afternoon, grapes had not seen the likes of me.

The barn gave off a stench. Even from just walking in its direction, I picked up the bloat of bad air. Heat prickled the backs of my ears. Tingle-stings, then a chill. I touched my finger to the soil, whiffed, and knew somebody had inflicted foul doings.

I approached the animal pen, real slow, not fully wanting to keep going but, at the same time, needing to know what damage had been done.

"Cakewalk!" I called out.

Rustled the feed in my bucket.

"Cakewalk!"

Turned my face to the swill of clouds now gathering overhead.

Silently begged my gosling friend to waddle his way out.

"Bird—come! Do your dance!"

But there was a hush in the pen.

I spotted Swank, Cakewalk's ma, writhing in the corner near a fence-tie, trying to breathe through the tiny holes at the top of her beak.

Our animals, all of them, were pleading.

Ash, our mule, struggling for any air.

Q, our sow, same way, but worse. Somebody had cut off her tail!

Stray, our cat, eyes rolled back under little slits of eyelids fighting to find life.

Patch, our cow, tongue hung out, asleep forever.

Still half-alive, Swank shifted, rolled. Showed me her child, my gosling friend, my Cakewalk, dotted with fleas, dead.

I knew right away what had happened. It was common in these parts. Neighbors warned us to watch out for the maggots of envy. Somebody, jealous of our little bit of good fortune, had poisoned and terrorized our farm animals. Our crops and land were infected, too, drained of the saps and juices that provided our livelihood.

That night, we gathered, trying to figure who'd poisoned our lives.

'Retta said, "Not likely it was Nate Gaston. He wouldn't taint his own property."

She explained how these kinds of mystery terrors were known to be inflicted by thems who want to hurt Colored people and our chances of getting ahead.

"They hate on us in the sickest ways." Faye shook her head.

Jo-Nelle nodded, agreeing. "It's a soul-sorry shame, but too true."

"I'm betting it was the Klan, committing their crimes on the quiet," 'Retta added.

For months to follow, fury clutched my gut.

Uh-huh, it had a mean hold on me. I was madder than mad. Pepper-red raced up the backs of both my knees, into that place between my shoulder blades, where anger rises, crackles, spreads to all my whole skull.

The ache I had from missing my animals wouldn't let me sleep. Days turned to nights, spinning, mixing, ripping at my skin from its underside.

Never mind that I don't spit seeds. My throat burned, forcing me to hack up balls of snot from the place where I swallow.

I couldn't even try to not cry. Mad-hot hornets swarming my insides stung my whole heart. It hurt so bad.

NIGHT-DEEP

WHERE AND WHEN: *Ruleville, Mississippi. Late December 1942. No stars. No moon. It is colder than cold. Roly plods with deliberate intention across the land, its frosted sheet crinkling under his feet.*

S PENT THE REST OF THE FALL SUMMONING MY WILL, nursing our farm. I was proud of what I was able to accomplish. Our turnips came back for a time. Yams, too, but as struggling roots.

It got worse. We had no livestock, save for a few sickly chickens who'd survived. You can't thrive without healthy fruits and vegetables, or when a farm is barren of animals. And nobody can stay free of sharecropping's web 'less their resources allow them to be truly independent. After the poisoning, we could not get truly free.

Winter soon came, bringing the cruelest cold, uncommon for Mississippi. I had no choice but to plunge headlong into a Night-Deep, the vigil to be endured after tragedy strikes the soil—the same laying in the fields I'd undergone as an orphaned baby, pressing my essence into tainted earth.

The Night-Deep wasn't for weaklings or scaredy-cats. It was a way to find healing, and to restore the land.

Through family tellings, I'd learned Night-Deeps aren't prescribed by no almanac. Being set down in a Night-Deep as a baby is different from choosing to put yourself in the middle of a Night-Deep. It was strong medicine for all souls who dared to face it. My own ma and pa, wanting better for me, had been brave enough to risk leaving their baby boy in the Night-Deep's uncertainty. Now, being somewhere near to age twelve, I had to summon my own courage.

'Retta warned me. She said I might die trying this.

"I'm a Night-Deep child!" I snapped. "Lived through it once, and will again."

Besides, I told her, our family was already on the road to dying. I *had* to try. We needed to stay alive.

'Retta begged me to find another way. Pleaded as I trudged toward the centermost place under the sky, on our slice of property, now cursed with the spell of prejudice.

'Retta worked hard to reason with me.

"Roly, there are no stars tonight. No moon, even. It's a frozen mess out here." She spoke fast, willing her words to hurry up, to somehow turn me back. "This ain't like when you were a baby. You didn't know no better then. You could have frozen to death, had we not found you soon after your ma and pa had placed you down."

I was set on my intention. No back-stepping, no.

Said to 'Retta, "It's because I'm *not* a baby that I'm gon' do this. I know better now that I gots to."

To bring back our snippet of land, I had to press myself

into its brittle skin. Starting tonight, I would sleep in the fields, for weeks if needed, seeking that poisoned earth's cure, not never turning back.

'Retta and I set out together, her arms filled with a quilt.

I walked purposefully, my feet taking their time. My heart and will deliberate, too.

Would not stop, no. *Could* not. Needed to find the right spot. Needed to follow the needle on a compass pointing the way from someplace deep inside me. I felt a forward tug at my belly button, something pulling me ahead.

When we came to a wide-open clearing, far from the house, I told 'Retta: *"Here."*

Sat cross-legged. Stayed.

'Retta wrapped all of me. Begged again I should return with her to our house. I shook my head. Refused.

'Retta cautioned, "When the cold numbs your bones, use some sense, Roly. Come home."

This had nothing to do with sense—common, horse, or otherwise. This was about knowing a truth that doesn't live in the same pen with sense. *This* was a way out of no way else.

I laid, turned onto my side. Curled myself inside myself. Let the land rock me in its winter rhythm.

'Retta waited as I settled, huffing into her cupped hands.

Steam rose from her short breaths. Before she left, she put her lantern to the tucked spot at my feet, pulled two blue strips from her pocket.

"Take these."

'Retta held out a pair of long knitted stockings. Looked to be my right size.

"Already got on socks," I told her.

'Retta was quick to suggest, "Use them for mitts."

She was faster still to fit the blue strips onto both my hands, yanking their tops up each arm, over my elbows. Those socks were softer than a piglet's belly. Smooth, too. And truly warm. In the toe of one, my fingers found a small, hard ball of comfort waiting for me.

"An amarillo agate," 'Retta said.

Told me 'bout that doctor's daughter, from when she was a child.

Told me 'bout the sapphire socks, knitted by her pa.

Told me, "Yours now."

FIRELIGHT!

WHERE AND WHEN: *Ruleville, Mississippi.
January–April 1943. Nearing midnight. Roly delivers
this piece wrapped in 'Retta's quilt. He's filled with
conviction. Strong. As he recounts this part of his story,
taking it from winter to spring, Roly steps out from
the quilt to gather flowers from an abundant field of
blossoms. His quilt now becomes a blanket of color,
ablaze with beauty. Roly creates a bouquet, tells of his
triumph, and his misgivings.*

DURING THE DAY, I WORKED LIKE ALWAYS. BUT I SLEPT IN that field nightly. Shivered for weeks under an entire moon cycle.

Recited what I knew from *The Old Farmer's Almanac.*

Waning.

Quarter.

Crescent.

New.

Waxing.

Full.

Thirty-one nights of cold, watching for change. Reaching for the moon's light. Stretching to believe in a new sky.

The field was a mix of hoarfrost and the hatred of strangers who had seeped their evil into our land's frozen soil.

If it hadn't been for the amarillo agate and sapphire socks, I'da been sucked into its clutch by frostbite.

I dreamed wild stories every night.

Haints and spirits visited my vision.

Men with no faces pouring snake venom from slop buckets.

Chickens flocking to feed, pecking, eating. Keeling.

Piglets suckling tainted milk from their poisoned mamas.

Me, a wriggling, hungry infant, found among shards of hay, hungry.

Even in the cold, sweat beaded my cheeks and neck. Among my nightmares, I wept. Tears and sweat stung my eyes. But I welcomed all that salty, trickling liquid. The serum, seeping into this tainted place, was the Night-Deep's way of cleansing the deadly earth.

On January's final night, the croup came to call.

Uh-huh, came with a malady's might!

I shivered, flinched. Looked into the face of an illness that could mean the end of my Night-Deep vigil. But soon I'd come to see this was the *beginning* of something.

I dared the croup's barking cough to keep it up.

I called out in the cold black, *"I ain't no kind of limp willow!"*

From a place in back of my belly button, pain came. A twisted ache that moved through all of me.

I squeezed the agate marble hard inside the sock.

Yes, *uh-huh*, I did, too.

Its warmth grew. Slow at first. Then swelled.

That's when I pulled what was a tiny surprise from its sapphire hiding spot. Sat up to see. Cradled this little ball in both blue mitts.

Then came the gift's wonder.

Firelight!

That itty bit of glass warmed my face. Lit my nose-tip and cheeks. Blazing hope!

Months later, spring's warmth brought its miracles. Or was it the power of believing? Maybe those were one and the same.

Finches played fly-and-seek, showing off their wings. These birds, red-headed and haughty.

Pear buds filled our trees. Blossoms came freely. And here come baby chicks parading behind their hens. Downy puffs as yellow as so many daffodils. All that bright, dotting our land.

Who knew there would be so many kittens, now running 'round the barn? Seven in all. A mix of calicos, tabbies, and spotted blacks, scratching after busy ants, who built their hills.

And wouldn't you know those kitties could dance? Not quite a cakewalk. But a shuffle, for sure.

I was proud of our daisies. Gathered them for our family supper table. Filled jelly jars with water from the well. Set the bouquets side by side.

Flowers, they can grow in the grittiest dirt. Through a tar-paved road, even. Blooms are hardy when healthy soil supports them. Same way for me, too.

TESS COLES

WHERE AND WHEN: *Ruleville, Mississippi.*
Summer 1945. Roly's hands are deep in his pockets
while he walks. Cicadas sing in the trees. Their chorus
puts a bounce in Roly's step. Barn swallows play
overhead, darting, flirting.

RETTA SENT ME TO BARDELL'S GENERAL STORE TO BUY A set of canning jars for pickling cucumbers. She gave me clear instructions. Held me by both shoulders to make sure I understood. Spoke firm.

"Find the jars. Pay. Leave. Don't dawdle on the way home. Keep your eyes front. Walk straight up the road."

I repeated to let her know I'd heard.

"Find. Pay. Leave. Walk."

"And what else?" 'Retta asked.

I bumped her shoulder to mine. "Don't dawdle on my way home."

I got to Bardell's soon as they opened. Tess Coles was there, working.

I'd seen Tess sometimes when we visited her church, the neighboring congregation, but I never truly took notice of her.

I guess you could say Tess and I met for real the day she climbed Bardell's store ladder, not once asking for my help. On this particular morning, she was cleaning the flour bin, blowing dust from its corners, sending a powdery sheet into the air of the small shop.

Her bony elbows and skinny wrists caught my attention. They moved with precision and rhythm, like the treadle on a sewing machine.

Tess had her face down in the flour bin, her back turned away, wiping. She didn't see me waiting to be helped. We were the only two in the store.

I called to her from behind. "Girl, you gots a customer!"

Those elbows and wrists were busy twisting a dust rag, determined.

"Girl, you're ignoring the patrons in this place!"

Tess shrugged.

I persisted. "Anybody work here?"

The elbows and wrists stopped quick.

Tess turned, sharp, her hair a powdered crown of flour dust.

She looked bothered. "We're not open yet."

"Your door's unlocked," I objected.

"Read the sign *on* the door." Tess brushed the white from her forehead. She'd tucked the dust rag at the waist of her apron.

She huffed. "Can't you see I'm busy?"

I huffed back. "Can't *you* see I'm here to buy something?"

I wasn't one for mouthing off to a girl. But this girl's sass made me feel some kind of special.

That's one of the things that caused me to look different at Tess, from when I'd seen her other times around town. She was all brass, this girl. Why hadn't I noticed before?

Tess Coles had a solid, shiny way about her. And grit.

I told her I was there to buy canning jars. As it turned out, the jars were on a high shelf, needing her to climb the rickety ladder leaning in a corner. She wasted no time, Tess. Hoisted that ladder, shimmied it across the floor, yanked it into place, and climbed with sure-footed conviction. Not once did it seem to occur to her to ask my help. Her shoe bottoms set me to worrying she would slip from one of the ladder rungs, or get snagged and fall.

Them were some timeworn shoes. One had its flat heel peeled half-off, looking like a dangling melon rind. The other shoe's sole was a mess of warped leather. None of that stopped Tess. She gripped each wobbly rung. Hung on. Kept her eyes fixed to the high-up jar shelf. Climbed.

I held the ladder secure at its bottom, whispered:

Don't slip....Don't fall....Don't crash....Don't splat....

I worked hard to push the sight of Humpty Dumpty out of my mind. Wouldn't that be something? Me, coming home having to tell 'Retta how I'd made a girl break her head open.

Tess called out from the ladder's top rung.

"How many jars you need?"

"How many you gots?" I asked.

She shot back, "What we *got*, and what you may need, are

two things different. What I *don't got* is all day to be up here waiting on you."

Tess was all about keeping to getting things done.

"Bring me down three jars, then," I said.

That made Humpty loom even bigger in my mind's eye. Tess had the jars secured in the crook of her arm while she climbed down, holding on with only one hand. I kept my eyes on her flap-heeled shoe, praying that floppy, rough-hewn scrap would hold.

Thankfully, Tess made it down in one piece. She secured the jars in a wooden carry-trough. Thanked me for my patronage. After that, I did what 'Retta had instructed. Paid for the jars, and left. I said a short goodbye to Tess, who was back to cleaning the flour bin.

On the way home, I had trouble following the rest of 'Retta's instructions. It was hard not to dawdle. I struggled to keep my eyes front and to walk straight. Distraction was having its way with me. I took a shortcut through Bardell's field, noticing the clover blooming, and got sidetracked by a turtle crossing a dirt path. When I found my way back to the main road that led home, Tess Coles stayed on my mind the whole time.

Around town, I noticed Tess more and more. Wasn't long

before I started finding reasons to visit Bardell's. When the yard fence needed painting, I was quick to get over there to buy the paint. When it came time to rewire the chicken coop, guess who volunteered to make the trip to fetch the wire?

Soon 'Retta caught on.

"What's at Bardell's?" she wanted to know.

"Chore supplies, is all" was my reply every time.

And every time, 'Retta's eyes rested on mine, not letting me look away. We both knew I was telling a half-truth.

I couldn't hide it for long. 'Retta and everybody else noticed I'd taken a liking to Tess.

Even though we'd been acquainted from when we were kids, it was as if I'd been given a special pair of glasses. I started to see Tess in a new way, not the same as before. It was different from when we was small children, our churches visiting each other and sharing picnics.

One Sunday, not long after I'd been making a habit of stepping over to Bardell's, we visited Tess's church. She got up from the pew and played piano to accompany our choir. Soon as I saw her fingers pressing self-assured rhythms into the piano's keys, I knew I would be spending my life with this girl.

It was right around then I put more time into making myself look nice for church, wetting my palms with warm lavender water to smooth wrinkles out from the one Sunday shirt I owned. Tess began to take special notice of me, too. By then, somebody had mended the bottoms of her shoes and scrubbed them with boot polish.

Once, for a choir come-together, when our church choruses joined up to sing, Tess came ahead with a musical mix of stride piano and gospel styling. Yes, Tess did.

Anybody who understands what's proper and right under the roof of a holy place knows stride piano is what's played at parties, not during prayerful moments. It was as if nobody had ever let Tess know this. She took to those bass notes with sure-fingered fury. Winked and nodded at me every time she filled the room with her handful of piano keys, ticking out breeze-chords and flatted fifths.

That's when Tess Coles walked into my heart, and stayed. It's when falling in love with her was what I did.

Come the next Sunday, I brought a special show-and-tell to share only with Tess.

There was no mistaking she felt the same about me. But here's where what people say is one of my limitations comes in.

I'm not for rushing things. I believe in slow-and-sure. As much as I loved Tess, I wasn't hurrying to make any rumblings about going steady. Why you gotta rush love? Affection is something that should move at its own pace. Like grass, it takes time to grow, don't it?

And so, I was not even anywhere near to hinting at getting hitched with Tess, come the future. I later found out that my slow-and-sure to make a full-on commitment wasn't sitting right with her. See, back in that time, when there was somebody you had eyes for, and them eyes kept returning to that girl, whose eyes met yours back, that was the beginning of talking about taking steps for tying the knot when you was more growed up. These kinds of conversations began as young as thirteen or thereabouts.

I'm guessing it was around that time Tess came to a decision. She was like that. Intentional. After months of waiting, come to find out, if I didn't ask her to marry me, *she* was gonna do the asking.

Being a proud person, I think Tess knew it could hurt my pride for a girl to be proposing, so she held off. But this girl, she didn't like to wait. Especially when something needed to get done.

Tess most likely bit down on her tongue and waited to see what I was gon' do, or whether to just tell me straight-out she wanted to be my wife someday. And she wasn't one for lowering herself for anybody, so choosing not to get down on her knee to propose probably gave Tess good reason to pause.

Near a year passed. I took a trip to Bardell's to get saddle thread. Like always, I arrived in the early morning, before the store was truly open. Tess unlatched the door. Let me in. Made sure the CLOSED sign was still face-out in the window.

"Can't wait no more on you, Roly," she said.

Now, as much as people accuse me of moving slow, I ain't dimwitted. Right then, I knew full-well that I'd better do what any self-respecting person would do who's coming up on being a man, who feels some kind of way for a self-respecting girl coming up on her womanhood. I needed to do what was good and right.

After church, I found Tess in the choir room hanging the chorus robes.

"I gots something I want you to see." I felt a smile rising in me.

Tess said, all haughty, "What is it, Roly? Some kind of jewel, I hope."

"Better," I said. "Close your eyes, hold out your hand. And," I teased, "for once stop mocking me."

Tess did like I said. Shut her eyes tight and put a button on that talkety lip she's got. Both her palms waited, wide open.

From my pocket, I lifted the amarillo agate marble 'Retta had given me during my Night-Deep. Gently, I placed the marble into Tess's open hands. She was quick to open her eyes. The marble's glow lit her skin's dark beauty.

"It's warm," Tess said. She could not take her gaze off that glistening ball. Curled her hands around the marble's heat.

She said, "It brings a song to my fingers—feels like fast piano."

I took both Tess's hands in mine. The marble's music pulsed in both of us. Two hearts in harmony.

Now, mind you, I'm a man of few words, but I mean what I say. And to Tess, I said, "This agate is ours to share. Love spreads out from the marble's middle. The music you feel in its warmth is how *I* feel about you."

I also told Tess nothing was more beautiful than a girl with strong convictions, and that her faith in knowing when it's time to do what's good and right had rubbed off on me.

Said *we* was good and right together, and that even though she climbed ladders with barely holding on, and even though I wasn't one for taking chances like that, did she agree that together we was meant to be?

Haughty Tess Coles, who is too talkety, softened. Nodded.

Held that marble tight-tight. Closed her eyes again. They danced under her pretty eyelids. Tess let the firelight's music fill her up.

She was hard-pressed to speak, but managed to find the one word I was hoping to hear.

Yes!

After that, we committed to getting married in the years to come, when we was a bit older. We made a promise to tie the knot, when the time was right.

The girl who could put happy heat on the piano keys now shared my firelight. Someday she would be my wife. Misses Tess Coles Little.

CHASING THE WIND

WHERE AND WHEN: *Ruleville, Mississippi.*
Warm days, 1950. Roly holds a bundled baby.
There is love in his eyes. Gentleness in his expression.
A tender way about him that turns to edginess
as he shares a hard part of his story.

TESS AND ME GOT MARRIED NEAR TO FIVE YEARS LATER, and were blessed with a baby girl. Tess let me name our daughter Aggie, after the firelight that shines through the glass of our amarillo agate.

Aggie came into this world with her eyes wide open, and a mouth for shouting good news. I know new babies can't talk, but Aggie seemed born for speaking up. Even as an infant, her little lips wanted to form words, eager to make a point.

Aggie's baby gaze always seemed to look toward the face of tomorrow, as if she was watching the future. It was Tess's idea to give her a simple middle name—one letter, *B*, to stand for *bold*.

Aggie B., our girl.

Before Aggie was born, I'd made a blanket lined with lace, hoping our child would be a girl, frilly and pretty.

I was the very first to hold that precious child. Before Tess, even. But I could not have imagined I'd be holding Aggie for both of us, after Tess got her heart set on chasing the wind.

Now mind you, I'd held piglets, kittens, and chicks, but didn't know the first thing about coddling my own baby. I learned quick, though, that two arms are best, and always support an infant's head.

I also found out that whenever I cradled our newborn, a warm swell filled me. The very sight of Aggie, looking so much like Tess, brought me to soft singing.

It was around this time that Tess grew restless, telling me how the three of us should leave the South, and travel up north to find a new life outside of Mississippi, and let's discuss it. To me, there was no *discussin'* to do. I gave Tess the courtesy of listening, but we always reached a tense place on what felt like a forked road when I told her right here is where we're staying.

Time and time again, I said, "No cities for me, or our girl, Tess." And I meant it.

All right, here's the point in my story where happiness and hurt start to grow in the same garden. It's something I don't like talking much about, or recollecting, or thinking on. It's painful. Not a good memory.

I'll try to tell as much as I can. And since recounting what-all happened with Tess is not what I like to do, I'm gon' keep it real simple.

Soon after our daughter was born, Tess came to me with a haversack in her hand, and dressed up like she was going someplace special. She looked as if there was an important appointment waiting for her to arrive.

I held our girl, embracing all how tiny she was. While Aggie slept, baby wheezes rose from her chest.

And here's Tess talking about how she loves me and Aggie more than anything in this world, but can't stay in Ruleville, on account of wanting more for herself than dirt roads and cabbage fields.

I asked her, "Why you keep bringing this up, Tess?"

It was clear she'd been thinking hard on what needed to be said. My child's ma had been mulling an answer.

"Roly, as I been saying, I want to go up north to live in a city where there's opportunity. I want to step out of my ordinary. To learn. Grow. Change."

After so much discussin', I couldn't help but wonder if a termite had chewed down Tess's good sense.

I shot back, heated, "You're chasing the wind, Tess. Any kind of growing can be done right here. With us. Aggie and me, *we're* your opportunity. And ordinary is a good way to be. Means your feet can grow where they's planted."

Tess then tried to convince me that taking Aggie with her was a good idea.

"No, this baby ain't going to no city, while you reach for a dream you can't see."

Aggie stirred. Woke suddenly. Whined.

I tried to calm her restlessness, but she got to fidgeting and suckling at the air, wanting the milk only her mama could give.

"How 'bout our baby girl?" I wanted to know. "What kind of mother leaves her newborn behind?" I was asking as much for me as I was for our own child, whose whimper had now flared to a loud tinny sound.

I could tell by Tess's few words that she had made up her mind.

"Need to, Roly," she said. "And best to do it now when Aggie is a baby, before she can truly miss me."

My words were a lot more than a few. I was tired of *discussin'*.

I said, "Where, exactly, you heading—up north?"

Tess, she didn't even have a plan or a place!

Just her *need to*!

That set my insides to full-on agitation. To sharp anger.

Tess insisted that her *need to* was for the love of our daughter.

Talking about, "The road to better is out there, Roly. I want to find it, so that someday Aggie will know there's more in the world than tractors, tired flies, and tobacco plants."

Tess claimed that her *need to* rose from wanting to be

something more than a worker at a store where the customers were farmers, mostly.

With our baby mewling in my arms, I said to Tess, "You *need to* feed your child, and stay put. And you *need to* be with your *farmer* husband. And, since you're so good at climbing ladders and getting to what's high-up, you *need to* climb *down* from your high-horse dreams of up north."

Tess didn't speak. She let my gasket blow. Gently took our infant to a quiet corner, fed her, held her, and returned our sweet bundle to my arms.

I was simmering mad by then, but didn't want my rile to somehow seep into the peace our baby girl had found in the taste of her mama's milk.

I lifted Aggie from Tess's arms. "How long you be gone?"

She didn't have no answer for that. Didn't say.

"You *ever* comin' back?" I asked.

Same like before, Tess would not commit to returning to Ruleville. But she did agree that keeping Aggie with me was how it should be. She hoisted her haversack onto her hip. Reached down in. Handed me a flat package.

"For our girl," she said. "When the time is right."

Tess Coles Little, the mother of our only child, walked

down the gravel path that led to the entry road of our property. She moved with a will, not ever letting her haversack slip.

The sun had brought copper hues to the afternoon. But my heart felt dark. Mad at Tess. Afraid for her, too. And scared for our child's future of growing up without a mother. As much as 'Retta loved and cared for me, I still had a mama-sized hole that never got fully filled. I didn't want that for Aggie.

Like a tide changing its mind, Tess's walking slowed.

You ever hear how a person goes down a road and don't look back? That didn't happen with Tess. Halfway past the pecan tree that marks the edge of our land, Tess stopped. She set down her haversack. Shaded her brow from the high sun. Glanced back at me holding Aggie.

Even from far off on the blurred horizon, I could see Tess tighten with uncertainty.

I saw her wondering whether to keep on.

I saw hesitation.

Indecision rose in me, too.

Should I plead with Tess?

Motion her back?

Or let her keep on so she could find whatever unknown hopes were pulling her away?

As much as I wanted Tess to turn around, as hard as I wished her *looking* back would lead to *coming* back, I knew full-well I didn't have the power to take away anybody's dream. Tess was chasing a nameless wind, and I wanted to harness it. You ever try holding on to a gust of air, or putting a stop to a squall? It is near to impossible.

Right then, Aggie started to cry loud enough to startle the birds. Her wailing brought my attention back to the moment at hand, that of tending to my child. I lowered my face to let my gaze meet Aggie's black-button eyes. She was swaddled in the lace birth blanket I'd crafted for her arrival.

"Hush now, baby Aggie."

I offered my pinky finger to pacify her crying. Let her tongue suck at my skin, like a tiny flower petal, licking and licking.

When I looked up, Tess was gone.

The sky, a bolt of bright blue, let the sun show off its whitest smile. That brought warmth, but not comfort.

See, even in the face of a copper sun, there's a truth I've seen too many times in my life.

Among bright sunshine, sorrow can hide behind the clouds and wait on the far-off horizon. After Tess had left, whenever I gently kissed my daughter's forehead, it was easy to believe in the power of good. But however hard I tried to push it away, there was always an unsettled bee vexing my insides.

With Aggie's mama gone, and after so much struggle of my own, I had to work at shrugging off the sting of what can come from the hands of hatred. I worried for my baby girl. And for Tess, out in a world, with no plan or place.

I wish I could say I had faith every day. But I couldn't keep from fixing my eye on the horizon's clouds.

It's like that here in Mississippi.

Mud mixes with Magnolia wishes, even when the sun shines.

BETWEEN THE BETWEEN

PRETTY MISSISSIPPI:
A TROUBLED BROTHER'S
SOLILOQUY

WHERE AND WHEN: *Ruleville, Mississippi.*
September 1955. Dusk. Out back at the Little home.
Roly, years later, a grown man, is seated in a rocking chair.
He's just finished reading a newspaper.
Folds the tattered sheets, sets them in his lap.
His tone is weary.

WHEN MISSISSIPPI'S MA AND PA NAMED THEIR BABY, THEY called her Magnolia. She was a beautiful sight. Magnolia later became the official state flower, and the whole place was known as the Magnolia State. So pretty, that place.

Pretty Mississippi got a nickname, too. Along with being named the Magnolia State, it came to be called the Hospitality State. That's right, Hospitality. But see, *uh-huh*, the Magnolia State, she was, at times, a terrible hostess. Depending on who came to visit, Miss Hospitality forgot to put out her welcome mat.

Still had a lot of charm, though. The kind of charm you only finds in Pretty Mississippi.

Speaking of pretty, the Magnolia State could sure turn some heads. She beckoned all kinds of folks with her sunflowers and fleecy cotton, dancing under puff-clouds floating in a bolt-blue sky.

Soon, though, when you looked up toward the bolt-blue, you could see that Magnolia, a white-on-white flower, had grown wings. She spread them feathers as wide and as high as the beaked creature that was one of her state symbols—the mockingbird.

Magnolia and the mockingbird flew side by side, along

with a new winged thing that had swooped into Pretty Mississippi. This ugly bird came to add its darkness to Magnolia's land.

That winged thing! Jim Crow was his name.

Meanest menace ever. Didn't take long for Jim to lay down his iron-feathered laws. Colored people here, White people there, and ain't no mixing.

We gets less, worse, half, none.

Negroes are separate and no kind of equal.

Jim, he called us inferior.

Called us second-rate.

Called us names not worth repeating.

That's right, Jim told us go 'round back to beg at the alley door.

That's right, Jim insisted we sit in the last seats on the bus.

That's right, Jim made it real clear if we was thirsty, over there was a rusty water fountain with our name on it—FOR COLORED ONLY.

Jim let us know *our* children didn't dare go to school with *their* children.

Make no mistake. At the gate of the Magnolia Hospitality State, the front door to any public place was only open to

White people. That gate was a locked riddle to this hate-riddled place.

Jim Crow put a name to the shadow he was casting over Pretty Mississippi. Called it *segregation*. In time, that pitch-black winged thing had turned Pretty Mississippi into something ugly.

Mississippi became a pretty nightmare. Her gardenias and fluffy cotton clouds were laced with hate. In the middle of everything that was growing from Magnolia's garden, there were fields and fields of forgotten flowers—dandelions.

These hot-hued pom-poms on a stem were accused of being flower-pests. But how can blooms so bright, so determined, be weeds? These was hardworking people like me, like so many daddies and sisters and sick-and-tired mamas, sticking to their convictions as their stuck-to-sharecropping grit helped them keep on.

Dandelions, forgotten flowers in the eyes of some, are forced to remember what it takes to summon enough strength to stay in the sharecropping game. To endure what it means to be blossoms who are just as pretty, but treated as separate-and-not-equal.

Even though ugly segregation had flown into Pretty Mississippi, there was so much to love. Still is. Mississippi has every reason to brag about her catfish, oysters, and cornbread. And when it comes to sugarcane, swallowtail butterflies, pecan trees, and bumblebees, the Magnolia State is truly special.

Part of Magnolia's pride and joy is the Mississippi Delta, a triangle of land between two muddy ribbons of water.

The Magnolia State is good at singing the praises of her homegrown music, the delta blues. *Uh-huh*, the delta blues is gut-bucket tunes that can fill up seats at a honky-tonk or jook joint. But that sad music grew out of sharecropper struggle. Why do you think we sing it so much?

Those delta-blue notes came from the wail of Black people so poor, they couldn't even afford enough *o*'s and *r*'s to spell out their poverty. Couldn't even borrow a letter from a friend, who was also worn thin, trying to make ends meet. Instead of saying we was *poor*, deprivation forced us to admit we was *po*.

When folks invite you to the Mississippi Delta, they're quick to crow about its plantations, front porches, corn pone, and fatback. What your tour guide won't show you is the Mississippi Delta's evil side.

Sometimes I think Jim Crow himself was hatched from an egg formed in the Mississippi Delta's bedeviled soil. An egg fried in racist grease and topped with home-cooked cruelty.

A month back, August 1955, Pretty Mississippi got her name in the Negro newspapers. But there wasn't no kind of pretty in the headline that read:

BOY, 14, FOUND DEAD IN MONEY, MISSISSIPPI.

His body was floating and bloated in the Tallahatchie River.

The child's crime was making eyes at a White woman.

Hooded men wanted to teach him a lesson.

For us Colored people, Mississippi is no kind of pretty.

Plain and simple, Mamie Till's son is now six feet under hatred's soil, while Jim Crow flies overhead, casting his wrath. But that child is not a forgotten flower. Emmett's memory lives on, brightly. The recollection of that child's legacy is as resilient as a dandelion's determination.

Yes, *uh-huh*, that's the state of this state's Hospitality. The sweet scent of Magnolia's blooms rise in the air, while fertile hatred lingers everywhere. That's the pretty nightmare that churns in Mississippi. That's the way a state can be two ways at once—pretty and vile.

Delicate flowers whose pretty petals try to hide what's

underneath the delta's muddy land. That's the mixed-up state of this state.

There's more, too. Mamie Till's son wasn't the only one. Our Negro newspaper is filled with stories about ropes around throats. About slipknots, cinched. About Colored boys gone missing. About husbands and fathers and brothers wrongly accused. About little girls last seen whirling in tall southern grasses, singing ditty-songs with Magnolia's mockingbirds.

Most evenings, I look forward to reading my Negro newspaper. I like to roll around in all them words and sentences. I like to let the power of reading roll around in me. But the Negro newspaper's stories sure bring home some foul truths. Its headlines remind me that sometimes there's a curse in knowing how to read. When my eyes land on what I wish I didn't have to see, it's impossible to forget what I've just read—the unspeakable dread of wondering, *Who's next?*

Used to be, I would read the Negro newspaper in bed before falling asleep. Used to be, I could turn those rattly pages, then turn onto my pillow. But I learned a hard lesson from doing that.

I started dreaming about those unspeakable acts.

I started spending the night with the mixed-up state of

the state of Mississippi haunting me with her pretty nightmares.

Sunflowers, honeybees, cotton fluff, and magnolias, all dancing in southern breezes next to Sir-Sir garter snakes with big teeth, playing ring-around-the-rosy with Jim Crow, and cackling. In my pretty nightmares, the beauty and ugly dripped together under the light of a misty Mississippi moon.

How many mornings have I tried to throw off those strange dreams?

How many nights have I laid awake, hoping the pretty nightmares would go away?

At the same time, I love my Magnolia State's cherry-bark trees. And night frogs that sing. And autumn mornings' pie-crust skies, rolling out as far as forever. And lightning bugs. And white butter. And washbasin music. And red carpet roses.

But for all its pretty, I can't ever escape Mississippi's state of mind that stays in *my* mind. You see, pretty nightmares are stubborn. Their stains won't come out, even in the light of day. Scrub all you want. When you're Colored and living in Mississippi, oppression is dyed deep in your being.

AGGIE B.
1962 to 1968

NEW DAY

High heat, coming ahead with a one-two punch.
An upper-cut to the chin.
But this center-stage slugger turns her cheek.

Races toward the hurdle.
Runs toward progress.
Raises her hand.

Volunteers for a scene-shift on discrimination's stage.
When others try to press her down by pressuring her
    to wear an apron,
    she won't dress as expected.

No frilly missy-miss. No fake curls. No, honey, this girl is real.
Her role is to bring it all home.
She's been cast to help others cast their votes.

Rebellious one, star of a show called Let Us.
It's her turn to speak.

While she gears up to enter,
Loretta looks on,
flap-flapping a straw fan, big as a gibbous moon.

Can she bring a breeze to her niece's eager ways?
Or does the flap-flapping serve to fan the fire?

This girl, her brother's child,
like a daughter to Loretta, is cut from the same
      spirited cloth.

She snatches the baton from the branches
of her family tree to win the race on race relations
      in the Magnolia State.

      But wait!

There's something to be said for legacy.

That playwright from long ago who asked us to explain
what's in a name, will tell you that anything other
than being true to who you are is not as sweet.

So here she is, for true — Aggie B. —delivering this
journey's final lines on why her bright name
speaks volumes,
as she ushers us to equality's election.

FOLKS CLAIM I GOT MORE NERVE THAN A BAD TOOTH. BUT there's nothing bad about being bold. *Bold* is part of who I am. Aggie B., that's me.

Say what you want about the way I'm bringing it. If it makes you happy, call my recollections running off at the mouth.

Or bearing witness.

Or speaking my mind.

And *speaking* of *my mind*, it is sharp, so I will tell you what was *on* my mind when I raised my hand.

Looking back, I'm thankful to the suffering I endured. It changed me. Made me so strong. I'm even grateful for the broken bones. For the bruises and wounds. My welts and hurts let me see deep into memory's memory.

When I close my eyes, I can still taste that pain. Can feel it, too.

Bam!

The ache is way far in, between my ribs. In back of the place where fear once settled.

With my eyes shut, I can also see the light of a new day, streaming through windows once clamped tight. I can hear the hush of early morning as it slips into scorching after-noons, whispers, rolls to dusk, calls crickets.

I'm supposing that by the time I'm done, my story will scorch, roll, sing, and then some.

What I've learned through it all is this:

If I dare to put my backside in the chair, and my hand in the air, change happens. Not being scared to raise all five fingers means I can reach past the pain of bruises and wounds.

I strike back by lifting high.

See, raising *is* reaching, way up.

NAMING ME

WHERE AND WHEN: *Ruleville, Mississippi.*
A spring evening at dusk, 1962. Aggie is alone, center,
surrounded by a blue-black sky, slowly darkening.
Fireflies dance as she introduces herself.

WE ARE THREE LEAVES FROM ONE TREE. SAME, BUT different. Aunt 'Retta and Pa Rollins raised me, they did.

How we made it this far living inside the same walls is anybody's guess. We sure do clash.

To most everybody who knows him familiar, my father, Rollins Little, goes by the name Roly, on account of his girth. He's always been Pa Rollins to me.

My father and I are curdled milk in tea. Sometimes when we're together, there's a sour separation between us.

Since as long as I can remember, Pa Rollins has been harping that I need to be more like every other missy-miss girl in this town. But the other girls around here are all daisies, set on rolling pie crusts, looking at mirrors, and turning their plaits into pin curls. There is not one of them I want to call my friend.

And what is the point of an apron? If you don't mess with cake flour, there's nothing to dust off your front. Besides, I'm no yam pie, all soft inside. I wipe my hands on my coveralls. Pa Rollins, he says, if I *tried* pin curls, I could be pretty. Me, I say, I *am* pretty—pretty ready to *not* wear a skirt or apron, or bobby pins, or socks, even. I'm not keen for putting anything on my feet. Pa Rollins, he makes me, being I could step on a rusted nail, or press out the protein innards of night crawlers we need for fishing bait.

And since we're on the topic of stepping and pressing, please don't go anywhere near asking me about my mother, because I only know what people say, and what they say by *not* saying. Even though Pa Rollins has never been shy about speaking of Tess, he offers just as much as he thinks I need to know.

Told me, said—he and Tess met, took a keen liking to each other, married, and had me.

Said—it was soon after when my mother decided someplace up north had a dream worth following.

Said—Tess left Mississippi. And me. For something called opportunity that she hoped to find in a northern city.

Told me, "That's all there is to it, Aggie. No more to say."

Aunt Jo-Nelle and Aunt Faye never much bothered with me, except to proclaim that history repeats itself, how my own daddy was also left behind by his mama and a father he never knew, and shouldn't I be grateful that at least *my* pa is here for me. Aunt Jo-Nelle, especially, liked to carry on about there's no use sitting around sipping misery tea, feeling sorry for myself.

This past year, they each married, later in life than most womenfolk. Then they moved on, Aunt Faye to Alabama, Aunt Jo-Nelle to Kentucky. Within weeks of each other, they left with husbands and croaker sacks, and took their bossy attitudes with them. Aunt Jo-Nelle was the first to go. When she made her way off our land, I whisper-lipped what I would never say.

My ma took that same road. Now she's forever gone. If I'm in the mood to drink misery tea, that's my business! Let me gulp down a glass of feeling-sorry-for-myself, brewed, iced, laced with lemon pulp and a tall straw!

On the day Aunt Faye left, I stuck out my tongue, and quick-sucked it back into my lips before anybody noticed.

Pa Rollins, Aunt 'Retta, and me, we live in a clapboard house, on what Pa Rollins says was once connected to property owned by the Gaston family, now long gone. Pa takes great pride in telling how he's kept our parcel of the land alive through his nurturance, and not giving up on it, even in dark times.

Aunt 'Retta's my mother now. Says she and me got what's called *same circumstances*.

Both grew up without a ma.

Both with daddies who stomp on what's sad by singing.

Aunt 'Retta puts it simply.

Says, "Same circumstances means we's close-connected.

We feel things alike, you and me. Our emotions bubble in the same pot. Our souls bloom in the same hues."

The Littles are a family of passed-down, go-tell-it stories. From the time I was old enough to speak and repeat, I have known we are people who've made our way by boxing cotton and looking past the uncertainty of *can't see*. We say what we mean, mean what we say, but we don't say it mean. We're courteous, but truthful.

Here's something else worth knowing about me and my family. My name, Aggie, comes from the firelight in an amarillo agate marble. The B. of my middle name is for Bold. It's that simple.

Pa Rollins says, soon as I came into this world, my eyes caught glints like that smooth shiny stone on even the cloudiest days.

Just two months back, on the morning I turned twelve, Pa Rollins gave me the agate that had belonged to him, a *firelight*, he called it. The marble looks like somebody lit a flame inside its glass walls and figured out a way to make the tiny glow stay stoked.

Pa Rollins told me, said, "Had this since what now feels like before the before."

Said, "Firelight is what shines in all of us, Aggie. It's the gift of believing."

There's another part to the marble: the knitted blue stocking where the agate's been kept. One of two sapphire socks, my pa says.

The marble called to me as soon as I saw it. But the socks did the opposite. I could not get with them. My feet aren't made for anything but skin. My soles are calloused and strong. Even though shoes and me don't get along, either, I do wear them, but only when there's frost.

Pa Rollins has tried his best convincing about the socks. Told me how Aunt 'Retta's daddy had knitted them, softened the wool, and if I put them on, I would feel and agree.

Said, "Aggie B., these socks are balm to your toe-jam."

Softened wool, pretending to be silk, is for missy-miss people who wear aprons. Even so, for all the whole sixty-and-some days I have been my age, I've slept with the agate under my pillow. It's my namesake, blazing.

FLOWER BUTTON

WHERE AND WHEN: *Ruleville, Mississippi.*
Easter Sunday 1962. Aggie leans at the front door
of her church, watching the other parishioners gather
after services. She's framed by simple stained glass
windows on each side.

THERE'S MORE WORTH KNOWING ABOUT MY PA TO understand full-well how so much struggle between us has happened.

Today at church, Pa Rollins got up and sang with the choir, something he only did on occasion. His slow baritone showed how Pa Rollins can be solid and gentle at the same time. Mixed in with my father's iron will is tenderness. Just like the two ways a cotton plant can be. Steady *and* soft.

Pa Rollins is bigger than most daddies. Husky, with a laugh that bounces from a round, deep place.

Weekdays, outside of church, it was Pa Rollins's job to cure meats by prepping them to be hung for smoking in the salt shed. It's why my father, big as a bear, always smells sweet, like hickory chips and pork musk.

Along with smelling nice, my pa takes his own sweet time on everything. And he's obstinate. Pa Rollins needs ten forevers to make up his mind or to step onto any path that doesn't lead to a place he knows full-well.

If what's ahead isn't clearly set out in my father's view, he is loath to walk. Crusted tree sap moves faster than Pa Rollins. Though he is good with farm tractors, he has only two speeds to his motor—slower-still and dead-stop.

Aunt 'Retta moves slow, too. But not for any reasons of being stubborn. Since from when she was a child, she's had a condition that gives a limp to her legs. The cane she carries is like a good friend. With it, she often steps ahead of most folks, including her little brother, my pa.

I know, it's not good to poke fun at your very own father. So let me say this. Pa Rollins is skilled with planting things, and he understands nothing worthwhile grows out of criticism. Not once has he ridiculed me. He always sees the best, and will point it out.

From the very first, he's called me quick-witted.

Says—I'm smart.

Says—I have the might of ten.

Pa Rollins is short on talking. And humble. He's a man of few words, but when he speaks, he's firm.

When it comes to giving gifts made with his own hands, my pa is generous. He takes pride in the oak-wood cane he carved for Aunt 'Retta, his brown bee honey, and the mint leaves he's grown on a small plot out back of Holy Name Baptist.

Today, being Easter, he was pleased to present me with a special gift. Thankfully, I wore a collared shirt to church. Never mind that I refused to put on a skirt. I was missy-miss on top, with dungarees on the bottom. That was good enough. After services, Pa Rollins came ahead with a nosegay bouquet, just for me. Pinned one of the blooms at the place where I'd lost a shirt button.

Said, "Aggie B., you're a flower, always growing."

DUMB DOUBT-Y

WHERE AND WHEN: *Ruleville, Mississippi. 1962.*
Aggie hangs wet laundry on a clothesline. She is
talking haughty. Between fastening clothespins to sheet
corners, her hands rest firmly at her hips.

DON'T EVER TELL ME SOMETHING CAN'T BE DONE, OR ISN'T possible because of a thing called Dumb Doubt-y.

That's right—*Dumb Doubt-y*. It's what nonbelievers cling to when they're scared of taking action. Dumb Doubt-y is uncertainty. Not being sure. Misgivings.

Dumb Doubt-y is ugly, smart, devious, and sneaky. It's the barking dog between your ears.

Dumb Doubt-y is powerful, too. It makes you believe *not* to believe in yourself. It has a way of inching up from behind when you're looking in the other direction. Dumb Doubt-y is more evil than a boll weevil. It eats away at what's possible.

And here's another warning. Dumb Doubt-y is at its very worst when it nips you from the inside, when it makes you feel *you're* dumb, or can't do something. Or that you're alone because nobody likes you, like runny coleslaw left at a picnic.

But, see, when Dumb Doubt-y comes around, I don't pay attention, because I know what I know what I know. And what I know is that Dumb Doubt-y ain't got a hold on me.

Since I know what I know, I was not going to hide it under Dumb Doubt-y's loud lies. Pa Rollins liked to caution me about being too mouthy. He didn't like me acting so outspoken at times. Said I should put a latch on my lip. Said know-it-all is not the way to be.

I always worked hard to keep from talking back to my father. Spouting off always made matters worse. Besides, I didn't need to argue or push. Because, in my heart, I *knew* that I know what I know what I know.

Yes, I *knew* that Aggie *do*.

THE RULES OF
DUE SOUTH

WHERE AND WHEN: *Ruleville, Mississippi.*
August 1962. A gathering place. Aggie peels open a
folding chair. Sets it down with a will, then sits, feet
firm. She's got a hand capped at each knee.

HERE ARE THE FACTS FROM TWO YEARS BACK.

Fact: Cassius Clay went into the ring, 1960.

He struck a blow by taking home Olympic gold, in Rome. Showed the world how a boxer could be undefeated. Proved himself by knocking out Dumb Doubt-y, who had come to Rome to set down fake limitations on what a Negro teen from Louisville, Kentucky, could do.

Fact: Wilma Rudolph. Same games—1960 Olympics. Same Dumb Doubt-y, prowling around, trying to turn believers against Wilma, who sprinted past Dumb Doubt-y's nonsense. Stormed to gold by running races on a fast track that showed everybody how an athlete born in Saint Bethlehem, Tennessee, could cross finish lines in record time. And I know *for a fact* that Wilma did not wear an apron to earn her gold medals.

Fact: Cassius, Wilma, and I come from three places on the map that make what is called the South's chimney. On a map, Kentucky, Tennessee, and Mississippi line up like a crooked smokestack, filled with a furnace of wanting to burn away the prejudice known in these parts.

I believe Cassius, Wilma, and me are connected somehow, arm in arm, moving together. Those two have put victory ribbons on their hometowns. But where I live is still far off the road, a place nobody ever goes.

Fact: Not many people visit Ruleville, Mississippi.

No sights to see in this pimple of a town, except for red dirt rising behind slow farm tractors and tired caterpillars sleeping on logs.

If you're lucky, you might catch a breeze, but there ain't much else that blows into this dried-up place.

Ruleville's as stagnant as swamp water, and sometimes just as smelly. The main stink from all corners of town is segregation. Plain and simple, Coloreds and Whites don't mix in Ruleville. And if you're any shade of brown, you best abide by the laws that keep Colored people down.

That's probably how *Rule*ville came by its name—we're forced to follow Jim Crow's *rules*.

We're *ruled* by segregation's thorny wing.

That's right. Bigotry *rules* Ruleville.

One night in August, when the moon had hooked itself onto a thicket of clouds, a man came to Ruleville to see the sights. He had made a special trip. None of us knew it then, but *we* were the sights he'd come to see.

We were his destination.

We were the circled spot on his map that told him:

You Are Here. In Ruleville.

We Colored folk—who called this dried-up-cotton-patch

pimple-town our home—were the reason this traveler's compass had led him due south to our church, where we'd been invited for a town meeting with these visitors.

Aunt 'Retta was all about it. She welcomed the idea of them, here to explore Ruleville. Pa Rollins was another story altogether. He was not quick to jump. I was someplace in between, arms folded, but eyes and ears open. Curious and *let's-just-see* at the same time.

It seemed Charles McLaurin didn't know none of the rules about Ruleville, because he arrived all eager, and ready to step past Jim Crow's shady ways. I felt sorry for Charles at first. He seemed ready to challenge all kinds of rules. That is not easy in this town.

Like rain when you don't expect it, Charles came on softly, then hard and unmistakable in his intention. He was a member of the Student Nonviolent Coordinating Committee. I'd heard about them from reading the same newspaper that reported on Cassius and Wilma. Charles and his friends called themselves SNCC. Said it like *stick*, but with the letter *n* running through its middle—*snick*.

Some considered SNCC uppity and too big-minded, because of their skinny neckties and pressed pants. Others called them the SNCC *siddity kiddies*.

Many were college students with dreams of changing the world. I admit, Dumb Doubt-y started to whisper right when I saw Charles. He looked smart, but clueless about the rules of Ruleville.

I shook my head—or maybe it was Dumb Doubt-y coming on stronger—and I thought, *Whatever it is you're peddling, it is too pricey for this town.*

Now Dumb Doubt-y was truly at work. I felt myself wanting to tell Charles to quit before he even got started. Wanted to warn him that he was speaking to mostly farmers who'd been beaten down by Jim Crow's feathers, and who didn't like to look too far past *can't see.*

When Charles started talking, I only gave him a speck of my attention. But there was something about the way Charles spoke that soon made me take the cotton out of my ears, press it into my mouth, and do something that is hard for Aggie B. Little—shut up and listen.

Yes, I like to talk. That's a good thing, too, because words are powerful.

But today it was time to let my ears and eyes do their job. Right then, it had all come down to four letters that spelled out an important word and a question:

The letters: W-A-I-T

The question: *Why am I talking?*

Charles's tone was serious. Seems that he'd picked me out of the group, because his eyes kept pressed to mine. It was as if he'd chosen to speak directly to me. Like *me* was the sight he'd come to see.

I silently disciplined myself with what Aunt 'Retta calls the set-aside petition: *Help me set aside everything I think I know.* That was all it took. My plea was answered quick.

As soon as I *set aside* my own prejudice, Charles's message poured down on me like a storm. In that room, it was so quiet you could hear a mouse tiptoe on a cotton boll.

Charles encouraged all the grown people to register to vote at the courthouse in Indianola, a town about twenty-four miles away, a place that was more racist than Ruleville.

Some people didn't even wait to hear what else Charles had to say. They got up and walked out. Didn't stick around for the rest of Charles's message.

Aunt 'Retta held tight to her cane and listened. Pa Rollins, his knuckles were bent around being stubborn. He was one of the nonbelievers, shifting in his seat. I put a hand on my father to keep him still. His restlessness was a sure sign he wanted to leave.

Aunt 'Retta curled her fingers around my pa's wrist and

squeezed hard. It's a good thing, too. Charles had more to say that I wanted to hear.

Charles told us about a mass rally, to be held at Holy Name Church, that would explain how voting could improve the state of the state of Mississippi.

Said, told us—the rally would be organized by SNCC and the Southern Christian Leadership Conference, who called themselves the SCLC, and whose president was Martin Luther King Jr.

RAISING MY HAND

WHERE AND WHEN: *Ruleville, Mississippi.*
August 1962. A church pew. Aggie is fidgety.

A FEW DAYS LATER, WE WENT TO THE RALLY. AUNT 'RETTA had somehow convinced Pa Rollins to come. Still, my slow-to-roll pa—who, under my breath, I was calling *Mister Molasses*—was moving at a slug's pace.

He did not want to ruffle Jim Crow's feathers, or stray too far past the rules of Ruleville. When it came to making changes, progress was not on my father's list of important things to do. But he came along, grumbling.

Said—about how *we women* need men to keep trouble from circling and moving in.

Told us, said—his reason for showing his face that night was to keep us safe.

As much as I know what I know, that Aunt 'Retta and I can take care of ourselves, I was glad Pa Rollins *showed his face*. I wanted him to hear what Charles had to say, *to* his face, and to all the faces at Holy Name.

The rally was packed with Colored people and even a few White folks. Soon as we got to that crowded room, I saw a seat up front. Like being in school, Aunt 'Retta and I sat near the first row, where there was no mistaking *we women*.

Even though I saved Pa Rollins a seat next to me and Aunt 'Retta, I had to wave him over. He came, but it seemed to take all night. That man did not want to be up close to where progress was happening. We helped ease him into the idea by sitting in the third row, rather than the front pew, like I'd wanted to do.

James Forman was the first to speak. These people, so eager to tell about freedom, had a thing for speaking right to me. James's gaze was the same as Charles McLaurin's. It was searing, and never seemed to let me unhitch myself. James introduced himself as the executive secretary for SNCC.

Please don't ask me what an *executive* is, because we didn't see folks with those kinds of labels in Ruleville. But *executive* sounds impressive, doesn't it?

Made me want to call myself the Little family *executive*. Couldn't help but wonder what Pa Rollins would've said if I'd told him that from now on, he needed to call me *Aggie, the executive*.

Well, James, the executive, explained that it was our constitutional right to register to vote. I thought I was hearing funny when James said that. Nobody had ever said Black people could register and vote. So how on earth would I know such a thing? And judging by the people shifting in their seats whispering amongst themselves, no other Colored folks from Ruleville knew it, either. My guess is, many of us probably didn't even think about *rights*. When you spend most days wondering if you can get by on one meal, there ain't much left in you to be thinking about *rights*. Besides, living in Ruleville, who dared to let their mind go down the road of *rights*?

As the rally continued, something strange happened. James asked anybody who was willing to go to the courthouse in Indianola to register to vote, to raise their hand. They might as well have been asking us to stand on our heads. The idea of registering to vote seemed just as upside down. It sounded like crazy-talk.

Even though a few White people had come to this rally, James must have known that mostly Black and White don't ever mix. But here he was asking us to shake it up. It was as cockamamie as inviting a passel of peppercorns to visit a city of salt.

Most everybody kept their hands pressed to their laps. They were afraid their bosses would fire them if they tried to vote. Worse than *being* fired, they were scared their lives would be set *on fire*, starting with flaming crosses propped up on their lawns. Or firebombs thrown at their homes.

Just as searing *as* fire, the residents of Ruleville had the hottest kind of fright there is. They feared they'd be burned by the flames rising up from the evil doings of the Ku Klux Klan.

As I listened to James, I wondered why I didn't feel even a little bit scared, but what was the point of being frightened? That's the other thing about Dumb Doubt-y. It makes you feel afraid, even though *I-know-what-I-know* can gently hold your shoulders and lead you forward. Whether Dumb Doubt-y is messing with your head or not, the truth is, feelings aren't always facts.

With not a single hand raised, I wouldn't even look at Pa Rollins. Didn't need to. I knew he was hoping *we women* would sit still. A peculiar thing happened right then. My fingers trembled without my permission. I tried to calm them down by lacing my thumbs, and squeezing tight. But that seemed to make both hands even more determined. The skin on my palms started to itch, too.

This rally was just like being in a classroom. A question had been asked, and I knew the good-and-right answer. There was no Dumb Doubt-y to talk me out of what *we women*, and everyone else in Ruleville, too, needed to do. Don't know how it's possible, but my hands got warm and cold at the same time.

And more itchy. And eager.

I twisted in my seat worse than when nature's pressing on my insides to get to the outhouse. Pa Rollins sat as motionless as a stone, but I swear he was doing some quiet-loud wishing this night would end soon, and that we could all go home, same as we came, without no kind of trouble.

As best I could, I balled both my fists, hard-pressed to keep still. You ever try to play a game to see who can hold their breath the longest? That's what it was like between Pa Rollins and me that night. I was holding on for the dear life of me. Aunt 'Retta seemed to be doing the same thing. She had both hands firm at the hook of her cane, clutching tight.

Finally, I couldn't stand it anymore. Really, though, it wasn't *me* who'd run out of patience. It was my hands. One of them had a mind of its own, and raised itself so far, I thought my palm and fingers would fly off the top of my wrist.

Before I knew it, I had my hand up as high as I could get it, waving it like a victory flag at a parade. I was one of the first to volunteer to go to Indianola to register to vote. I knew that being only twelve years old, I was too young to register to vote. But my hand didn't care about the age a person needed to be to help make things better. Pa Rollins, he didn't speak, but scolded me with angry eyes. His look cut to Aunt 'Retta, who was staring back at her brother, full-on rebuking him with a sharp stare.

Here's where intention met up with serendipity, and the most surprising thing happened.

James and Charles asked for others to help spread the

word by traveling on buses to states like Louisiana and Texas. Well, you can best believe that, although some of us wanted to see things change, not many Mississippians were ready yet to travel to Texas, Louisiana, or anyplace too far away. Staying inside the state was about as much as we could expect with the people from Ruleville. If it were left up to me, and I was old enough to do whatever I wanted, I'd take a trip from Mississippi to Kingdom Come.

But listen to this. A White lady, sitting two rows in front of us, raised her hand as high as I'd raised mine. She volunteered to travel to places other than in Mississippi.

I saw it then, *waving at me*—the beet-colored blotch on the back of her hand. It looked like a beet-y butterfly, eager to spring from the lady's skin, ready to flutter to someplace high-up. The sure sight of it had caught Aunt 'Retta's attention, too, and she quickly raised *her* hand.

Told me, said, "Aggie, help me up."

She steadied herself on her cane.

I wiped both palms on the

thighs of my dungarees. I helped Aunt 'Retta to her feet, stood beside her while she spoke to everyone gathered.

Said, "My Aggie B. and me, *we women*, will go to Indianola."

Me, I blurted, "Yes, along with the men, *we women*, we will."

After the meeting, I waited near the door with Pa Rollins, watching those who had not volunteered leave out.

Aunt 'Retta and the White lady exchanged words that were brief, but looked to be friendly.

Later, back at home, Pa Rollins went to bed with not even a single good-night to me or Aunt 'Retta. There was scorn in his silence. The door to his room whined softly while closing behind him.

Aunt 'Retta explained that after a long time of working from *can't see* to *can't see*, distrust starts to blind you entirely, till all you *can* see is nothing changing. This had happened to my father.

When I asked Aunt 'Retta if she knew the lady with the blotched hand, she nodded.

Told me, said, "A salutation from my past."

GO-TELL-IT TIME

WHERE AND WHEN: *Ruleville, Mississippi.*
August 1962. The next morning inside the Little home,
Aggie and Aunt 'Retta are each in a chair. Aggie's arms
are folded tight. Aunt 'Retta leans forward on her cane.
Pa Rollins faces them. The mood is tense.

P A Rollins sat me down. Aunt 'Retta, too, like we were up-jumpy children having to mind him, and here was our punishment for misbehaving.

Looked like he'd seen a haint and a hornet's nest in the same nightmare, and had been stung by a swarm of Dumb Doubt-y.

My father had fright filling his whole face. Anger, too. He wouldn't look at me or Aunt 'Retta. What he did was walk the floorboards, near to stomping, restless. Anger brewing.

I didn't have to ask, because I knew.

But still, I said, "Pa, what's got you?"

His words had heat on them.

Said, "The two of you, you acting foolish."

For a man who most times don't talk much, Pa had a lot to say.

Said—going to Indianola was a mistake.

Said—bad would come calling if we took that trip.

Said—we were inviting trouble.

Said—Colored folks been killed for speaking up.

Said, "We don't need to register to vote, because it ain't gon' make no difference, no how."

Told me, "You're my child."

Said—I was acting like my mother, chasing the wind, and

more and more resembling her with freckles coming onto my lips and cheeks, and my forehead the same as Tess's, arched high.

Told Aunt 'Retta, said, "Sister, you leading my girl down a bad road. Stay home."

Told me—he'd made up his mind.

Right then, something else happened, too. The devil of opposites went to work between Pa Rollins and me.

The more Dumb Doubt-y buried itself inside my father and dragged him down, the more *I-know-what-I-know* got ahold of my soul, and led me ahead. Pa Rollins was being pulled under, while determination pushed me forward.

I knew that I knew I was not put on this earth to be timid. I believe there's something on the other side of Dumb Doubt-y.

You'd think from me being his child, Pa Rollins would understand full well that his daughter doesn't shy back for nobody. As the morning grew hot, bringing its swelter to our small house, Pa Rollins explained what he'd suffered as a boy, and how back-talk around White people brought hate. Took me through his memory of when, as a child, he'd endured a Night-Deep, on the same land, right outside our window, near to twenty years before.

This added to my list of reasons Aunt 'Retta and me needed

to go to Indianola. I thought hard on whether to bite down on my tongue and wait on Pa Rollins's storm to pass, or if I should just tell him straight-out what I needed to say.

That chair was pressing too firm at my backside. I stood up. Met Pa Rollins face-on. Pounced both my hands onto his meaty shoulders. Stopped my pa from his back-and-forth on the floor.

It was my turn to talk.

I told *him*, shouted, "No wonder my mother left Ruleville! There is too much stupid in this place. If grown Colored people can vote, maybe Tess will come back."

I told *him*, "Look closely at how we live. Don't have running water or a toilet even, because we can't vote for how life could be better for Colored people. I'm sure my mother sits pretty on her toilet wherever she is up north, and can flush after she goes! There are no outhouses in northern cities, I bet you."

I told *him*, "How we ever gonna make things better, unless we take hold of our rights?"

I told *him*, "I'm not old enough to vote, but the decision to help people register is *mine*."

Pa Rollins started to pace again, bull-mad now.

Aunt 'Retta rose from her chair with a will. Faced Pa Rollins, close-up.

She told *him,* "*We women* got our own minds to make."

She told *him,* "Back it up, Roly."

Then, with a woman's touch—kind, but firm; caring, but make-no-mistake—Aunt 'Retta pressed my father into the empty seat next to me.

Said, "Brother, it's go-tell-it time."

Said—we needed to speak to people about their right to vote.

I saw Pa Rollins bristle, then settle.

Saw confusion and powerlessness rise in his eyes.

Saw him forcing back grown-man tears.

Saw his stout body surrender.

Pa Rollins hung his head, his brow sharp-creased.

I went to my pa, hugged him, and could feel all his whole body trembling.

He looked right at me, eyes soft.

Kissed gentle on my forehead.

Said, "Aggie B., I loves you."

BROWN CHILD LULLABY

PA ROLLINS'S UNREST

WHERE AND WHEN: *Ruleville, Mississippi.*
*A few days later. A thumb-print moon hangs low, its
yellow smudge pressed in the warm night sky. Pa Rollins
is seated at the foot of Aggie's bed while she sleeps. He
lovingly strokes his daughter's hair, singing softly.*

Brown baby girl,
will you ever truly know?

Pa's eyes are watching this world.
Oh, how Pa's eyes are watching this world.

Brown baby girl,
holding you close.

While these eyes watch and wait
while this papa's gaze
stays on a new tomorrow.

Brown baby girl,
as this pa sees you grow,
will you ever truly know?

Will you ever truly know?
Brown baby girl,
your ma's love paves the road.
As we look.
As we hope.

Our child-sparrow,
brown daughter, mine.

Sweet child, sweet.
Sleep, child, sleep.

Brown baby girl,
can you ever truly know?

Pa's eyes are watching this world.
Oh, how Pa's eyes are watching this world.

ROUND TRIP

WHERE AND WHEN: *Indianola, Mississippi.*
Late August 1962 to fall 1963. Aggie fastens a buckle
on the bib of her overalls. Chin lifted,
she is ready for a trip.

S OMEBODY MUST HAVE KNOWN AGGIE B. ONLY SITS UP front, because even though the bus to Indianola was mostly filled, the first seat was free, right near to the driver. That seat looked like the wide-open hand of the sky inviting me and Aunt 'Retta to settle on its palm for the ride. Aunt 'Retta had carefully tied the tethers of her head-scarf, the periwinkle one she only wore for special occasions. She was dressed to greet. I was the only child in our group, there to witness and help Aunt 'Retta and my Ruleville neighbors any way I could.

Soon as we got to the courthouse, I saw the sheriff. His fingers rested on his gun. Near to twenty of us had come to Indianola. We stepped up right to where the sheriff was. We told him we were there to register to vote. He would only let us enter two people at a time. The flies were out, bobbing in humid winds.

Even though I like to be the first one, and up front, the sheriff picked who could go in. He told me right off no kids were allowed, and that I could only enter with an adult.

We had to wait for hours till our turn came. Standing out there on a day as hot as Tabasco sauce, I sensed something shady. All the whole time, the sheriff had his nose crinkled like there was a bad smell someplace. Most likely, he was catching a whiff of his own intolerance reeling back at him.

Finally, Aunt 'Retta's turn came. Inside, a sign hung above a bald man's head. The sign said who he was—REGISTRAR.

From behind the desk, the registrar brought out a book as big as a Buick. He was a beanpole of a man, skinny as a stick. Couldn't hardly hoist that book, let alone carry it to where we were standing. That's maybe why he had so many sweat stains on his shirt. The registrar was struggling to hold on to that big book. Needed both his arms underneath that thing to keep from dropping it. All the whole time, his face was flushed. Same for his neck. It was red.

Then—*brrrump!*

The skinny-stick man with the flushed face and hot neck let the book drop onto the table.

Told Aunt 'Retta if she wanted to register to vote, she had to first pass a reading test, and also tests that required written answers. He said it with a smirk, like he knew he had us over a barrel.

Aunt 'Retta, being honest and humble, said to the man, told him, "I ain't ashamed to say I don't got a whole lot of formal education. I'm smart, but rusty with hard reading. Had to leave school when I was eleven."

As much as it's good to be humble and honest, I wish my aunt had not admitted to that man so much about what she can't do when it comes to things like schooling, because he looked pleased when he heard this.

So all right, that man's attitude made me more determined to help. Even though Aunt 'Retta couldn't read good, I had been blessed with strong skills when it came to words in books.

But anyhow, I also got enough smarts to know I can't read *every* word, especially long ones.

Seeing as my aunt's humility is understanding what you can and cannot do, and seeing as how I know what I know what I know—I *know* I *can* read, and would now have to help Aunt 'Retta by reading as best I could.

Most of the others who'd come to Indianola were sharecroppers who, like Aunt 'Retta, had to quit school when they were young children. Like Aunt 'Retta, many folks in our group couldn't read, either, except for maybe a few word-snatches.

I was ready for anything the registrar man had. He opened the book at its center. Made more noise with that thing—*brrrump!* Let one heavy side fall onto his desk. Pointed at some thick pages. Said Aunt 'Retta had to read the sixteenth section of the Mississippi State Constitution regarding de facto laws, explain to him what it all meant, and then give some written answers, too.

Told me, "These tests are supposed to be taken alone, not with no assistance. But help, girl, if you want. How much could a child like you know anyhow?"

Soon as I looked at those twisty-long words, I knew it was more than our reading that was being tested. As much as I didn't like math tests or spelling bees at school, I was smarter than most kids my age. But *whew*, I was not even close to untangling some of what was on those pages.

I'm guessing most lawmakers, and even Jim Crow himself, couldn't have read or understood those knitty-knotty words. How did they expect people who'd grown up as sharecroppers and hadn't gone to school past the fifth grade to be able to make sense of those pages?

Aunt 'Retta looked at me with tired eyes. She knew I didn't have the slightest clue about those words, and neither did she. There was no mistaking it. Our patience was being put to a test much harder than any test these people gave us. That made me want it even more.

Seeing as reading from the book was only part of the test, next came sheets of paper with questions on it, like an exam at school. We had to answer the questions by writing on the pages. I figured this might be easier. I'm good at writing answers.

But even the instructions played tricks on my mind. And the tests were timed. We had ten minutes to answer a bunch of silly questions.

I started by reading the instructions to Aunt 'Retta. The registrar man watched the wall clock as we worked.

INSTRUCTIONS:

Do what you are told to do in each statement, nothing more, nothing less. Be careful. One wrong answer means failure of the test.

1. In the space below, write the meaning of the sixteenth section of the Mississippi State Constitution regarding de facto laws that you have just read.

2. Draw a line around the number or letter of this sentence.

3. Spell backwards forwards.

4. Print the word vote upside down, but in the correct order.

5. If the mayor of Mississippi dies, who succeeds him? And if both the governor and the person who succeeds him die, who can exercise power in the court of law?

6. In the first circle below, write the last letter of the first word beginning with "L".

It didn't take a genius to realize most of the test questions were gobbledygook that made no sense. Even the stupidest person knows a mayor runs a town, not a state. So there's no mayor of Mississippi.

Seeing as I had to read each question five times, we didn't get very far before the registrar told us our ten minutes were up. The pits under both my arms had gone all-wet. Same for the place on the backs of my legs where my knees bent. Sweat was having its way with me today. Even my wrists and ankles had gone damp. My scalp tingled, too. Itchy from thinking so hard.

Not a single one of anybody from Ruleville passed the reading test. The registrar was fast to tell us we had all flunked. Some of the folks who'd traveled to Indianola wanted to give up right then. Not me. Even though we failed to understand what was in that big book and on those cockamamie pages, I knew I'd passed an even bigger test—the test of outsmarting Dumb Doubt-y. I refused to let that sly hound come after me.

On the drive home to Ruleville, Aunt 'Retta snapped

open her pocketbook, unfolded a rumpled bunch of paper, smoothed the pages onto her lap, tap-tapped the top page with a firm finger.

Said, "Aggie, read!"

She had stolen a copy of the test.

Aunt 'Retta caught me blinking fast, knowing I knew what she'd done.

Said, "This is a free government paper available to all tax-paying citizens. I pays my taxes. I *am* a citizen. Stop looking at me like I'm a thief—read!"

I nodded.

Aunt 'Retta's stern smirk showed me there was no room to disagree.

Told me, said, "And besides, if something is free, you can't steal it. We gon' study these tests till we learn what it takes to pass."

I tried to explain to Aunt 'Retta that every test had different questions. That if we went to the courthouse again, there would be a new set of pages. Tried to tell her, too, that most of the questions were made-up and, no matter what, couldn't be answered. Aunt 'Retta wasn't having it.

Said, "Well, smarty, here's some questions for you. Are you a Little?"

I nodded.

Said, "Are we people who quit when asked to walk backwards, draw a line through stupidity, or vote standing on our heads?"

I giggled. Shook *my* head. Tossed a funny question back to Aunt 'Retta.

Asked, "If Jim Crow dies, who succeeds?"

She and me answered together.

Said, *"We do."*

Meanwhile, everybody else on the bus was cursing the registrar, and saying we all should give up now. Not me with that, neither. I was not about to let Dumb Doubt-y convince us to quit. People were all grumbling how the test wasn't fair, and that White folks didn't have to know about the sixteenth de facto of anything to register to vote, and that White people who couldn't read a lick were allowed to register.

I'm just glad a neighbor lady, Miss Fannie Lou Hamer, brought her fortitude. She was just like Aunt 'Retta and so many others on that bus. Fannie Lou was a sharecropper child, now grown and ready to make some changes in a cracked system of equality.

To lift us out from Dumb Doubt-y's clutch, Fannie Lou started up with "This Little Light of Mine," one of my favorite songs. All the other passengers couldn't keep from singing along.

I'm glad we got to singing, because we were tested again when the police pulled us over.

Said—we were violating the law by riding in a bus that was too yellow!

Said—our rickety-ride cotton-picking bus could be mistaken for a school bus, so we were breaking the law. The policemen charged our bus driver, made him pay a fine for the color of our bus.

Ain't that the silliest bunch of hog-slop ever? It's the gospel truth, though. Really. Not even the best tall-tale tellers could make this hog-slop up!

CAN'T STOP AGGIE B.

WHERE AND WHEN: *Back in Ruleville, Mississippi.*
Autumn 1963. Aggie walks along a dusty road,
recounting this piece of her story.

WHEN WE GOT HOME, PA ROLLINS WALKED UP SLOW. HAD sorrow in his eyes. Gathered my cheeks in his big hands. Tilted his forehead to mine, did something I have never seen him do.

My pa lowered his face, and started to whimper.

When Pa Rollins spoke, it was through an ache that had wrapped itself around him. His tone was quiet, heavy.

Said, "'Retta, word's out about you and Aggie making trouble by going down to register to vote. People saying my sister and child need to be stopped. Saying we better watch it. Saying to quit with your voting ideas."

Pa Rollins pleaded with us both, but especially with me.

Said, "People around here aren't ready for any of what you're doing."

Right then, a swarm filled my insides. It was as if a mosquito nest had been shaken open, and those needle-nosed bugs were all stinging at the same time.

Seeing Pa Rollins looking like the grit-will had been stolen from his soul, and how my bear-strong pa was weakened by what fear can do—*that* stung *me*. The hatred had brought fear, an evil thread stitching itself into my pa, and weaving a monster in his mind.

But, here's what I know. Love is bigger than any haint, spook, or monster. And when love and fear are trying to fight their way into the same heart, that heart is sure to break open, because the two can't fit in the same place. If I'd had any money of my own to spend, I would have bet my father's heart was being stretched, only he didn't know it.

I was not about to back away now from our dream of registering people to vote.

My face ain't good at hiding what's going on inside, so I'm guessing Pa Rollins saw the defiance in my eyes.

That night, Pa Rollins made us gather whatever we could carry and leave home. If we wanted to stay safe, we didn't have much choice. I took three things. My amarillo agate. My sapphire socks. And my only pencil, chewed down to a nub.

I'll be honest. As sure as I was that trying to help people register to vote was the right thing to do, I'd be lying if I didn't confess that Dumb Doubt-y started to nip at me as we made our way. Aunt 'Retta struggled to walk, and her breathing came hard and rattly as she worked to keep moving. Pa Rollins tried to shrug off the ache he was feeling inside. But all you had to do was look at him wincing to know worry had wrapped itself around my father.

As we silently walked, I was feeling my own heart's

tug-of-war. Pure and plain, it was that same heart-pull that was making me want to fight.

That was one of the scariest nights ever. And one of the darkest. We didn't fully know where we were going *to*. Just that we were leaving *from* the place where I'd lived all my whole life.

Seemed like morning would never come. I thought about Cassius Clay, throwing a black eye at injustice. And Wilma Rudolph, who not ever looked back or down as she raced toward a finish line that was up ahead in the dusty distance. Aunt 'Retta and Pa Rollins deserved gold medals, too. They stayed strong through weak limbs and throbbing.

With a black sky folding in and around us, I remembered that you can only see stars when the sky is darkest. That was the twinkle that kept me going. If Cassius and Wilma and Aunt 'Retta and my pa could keep on, so could I. *They* were stars in this darkness, lighting my way.

Kind strangers took us in. We didn't own much of nothing, but we had each other. That's what mattered most.

Seeing Aunt 'Retta and Pa Rollins so weak and tired, watching their spirits wither under the weight of segregation, made me know I needed to keep standing up to Mississippi's lopsided laws.

Soon as we settled, Aunt 'Retta somehow got ahold of the Mississippi Constitution, and studied its laws as if our breathing depended on it.

Night upon night, and sometimes *all* night, we reviewed those convoluted words and sentences. I underlined and struggled to make sense of anything that looked to be filled with letters twisted together like chicken fence wire, blocking off my eyes and mind to any kind of *know-what-I-know*. I didn't fully understand some of the words and ideas, but I was now reading a heap about constitutions and something called the Confederate Congress, and how stars on a flag can represent places where slavery was the way of the world.

Aunt 'Retta and me, we pitched test questions at each other to see how fast each of us could catch. Our questions were real, not fake. Studying could only help get us ready, somehow, some way, no matter what the test threw at us. I started the asking, then we switched off, with Aunt 'Retta asking me.

Me: "Throughout its history, how many constitutions has the state of Mississippi had?"

She: "The state of Mississippi has had four state constitutions. The first one from 1817, then 1832, 1868, and the one we got now, from 1890."

She: "There are how many stars on the Mississippi state flag, and what do they represent?"

Me: "Thirteen. These stars are part of the flag's Confederate battle flag, which has the number of stars that represent the thirteen slaveholding states that were part of the Confederate Congress."

Me: "What is a de facto law?"

She: "A law that's real in the eyes of the government."

She: "What is the most abundant crop in Mississippi?"

We: *"Cotton!"*

AS IT TURNED OUT, WE WENT TWICE MORE TO THAT HOT-AS-blazes registration place in Indianola. I held Aunt 'Retta's hand while we waited to go in. Both times, Aunt 'Retta flunked the test. Both times, we left with our heads up, single-minded about passing the test when we returned.

Aunt 'Retta, she asked, said, "Aggie, do you know what smart feet are?"

I shook my head. "Nope."

Aunt 'Retta explained, said, "Smart feet are those that walk away from negativity."

Told the registrar, said—we'd be back every thirty days till Aunt 'Retta passed his knitty-knotty exam.

We did show up again, and again after that. Waited for hours to take the test, and every single time, when we were called, I went into the examination room with my aunt.

Whew, I ain't gon' lie—those questions were harder than hard. By the fifth time of taking the test, I could tell anybody who asked me about *de facto* this and *constitutional* that, and every stitch that sews together the laws of Mississippi and the state flag.

Finally, Aunt 'Retta passed that test on the sixth time! Even though *she* took the test, I left there feeling *we* passed it together.

I am proud to say my aunt Loretta Little was one of the first and only Colored women in the county to register to vote.

SQUIRRELS

WHERE AND WHEN: *The Little home,
late fall 1963. The sun's setting glow bends long light,
crisscrossing behind Aggie, who stands tall. She hoists
an oversized jar filled with coins. The money is near
to overflowing. Aggie, arms firm around the money,
speaks with authority.*

A S SOON AS WE EARNED US A LITTLE VICTORY, IT WAS yanked away, taken out from under where we were finally able to stand firm on our accomplishment.

See, it's one thing to get the *right* to vote, but as I quickly found out, being allowed to actually cast a ballot was something else different. When we went to the polls to vote, the officials told us we could only vote if Aunt 'Retta paid the state poll tax. They were especially happy to tell *me* this, because they knew for certain I didn't have the money. Neither did most everybody from Ruleville. They were also pleased to remind us we'd be prevented from voting that day, or any day.

Well, tax or no tax, we'd come too far to step back. We started to save right away. When anybody asked me how we planned on getting enough to pay the tax, I showed them my money jar, gave them a front-row seat to *how*.

Welcome to the Little Family's Bank.

I'm Aggie B., your teller.

Come up close to the window so you can hear me good.

So this teller can tell you like it is.

Want to know how my family and me are making the poll tax money happen?

We scrimp, save, collect, deposit.

Count our funds daily.

Tally them up in our Poll Tax account.

Watch the totals rise in this jar, filling to the brim with our dreams.

Like squirrels, we sock it away.

We're frugal.

Always been like that, but even more these days.

We mix our meat with shredded bread to make meals go farther. To make meat last way past Friday.

What we don't spend, we squirrel away in the Little Bank.

Penny-wise. Thrifty. Careful. Prudent.

Every coin counts for the Poll Tax account.

The Little Family Bank thrives mostly on copper and small-change silver.

If we're lucky, a quarter will come into our hands for adding to the Poll Tax stash.

Since money doesn't grow on pecan trees or any other plant, we squirrel every chance we can.

Fifteen cents…

Twenty-seven…

Forty-eight…

Ninety-two…

Piling pennies. Small silver stashes.

The true bounty is in the roots of our longing.

Reaching for almighty dollars that will add up to the funds to pay for what already belongs to everybody else but us—equality.

Even as your head teller in the Little Bank, I wonder about the true meaning of the money we collect.

You ever look closely at coins?

Here's what I want to know from the presidents whose heads appear on all that metal.

Mr. Lincoln, Mr. Washington, Mr. Jefferson, do you know your faces greet us whenever we save and cautiously spend?

Mr. Washington, Mr. Jefferson, I guess you've been stamped on our quarters and nickels because you're America's founding fathers. But after you founded our nation, then what?

Do you know Colored people are lost in segregation's struggle?

And since, from studying for so many voting tests, I know that I know that you, Mr. Jefferson, signed the Declaration of Independence proclaiming all men are created equal. What did you mean by that? And what about we women?

Mr. Lincoln, being on the penny, I see your face more than any other president. So here's what Aggie B., your head teller at the Little Bank, wants to know from you.

When you issued the Emancipation Proclamation, taking the

*first steps to try and make it official that all enslaved people are for-
ever free, what were you thinking the word* free *means, even though
freedom didn't come right away for people living in slavery?*

To all three of you dead presidents, do you know your coins have
In God We Trust *stamped on their front?*

Do you know the word Liberty *runs near to each of your heads?*

IT TOOK SOME TIME, AND A JAR FILLED WITH AS MUCH *IN GOD
We Trust* as we could collect. We saved and saved those good
words and that money, and one day counted out enough of
what was needed to pay the poll tax. Gave every last cent to
this cause.

Finally, Aunt 'Retta and several others from our town
became registered voters, who *could* vote. And who *did* vote.
After that, I promised myself I would help as many Colored
citizens as possible do whatever it took to cast *their* votes into
America's ballot box.

COTTON CHRISTMAS

WHERE AND WHEN: *Ruleville, Mississippi.*
December 1963. Aggie leans on a beam inside
her house. She looks glad to be back.

N TIME, WE MOVED BACK TO OUR HOME, PRAYED EVERY night for safety and peace.

After putting up with so much, was I ever weary!

Thankfully, Christmas wasn't far off. The holiday season softened the upheaval that had shaken our lives.

Each night, we sang "Go Tell It on the Mountain" in the way it was written for Christmas, to announce the coming of the all-holy baby.

Go tell it on the mountain
O'er the hills and ev'ry where
Go tell it on the mountain
That Jesus Christ is born.

That hymn always brought the glory of a new day. And also, too, there were holiday carols about sleds and snow.

Now, anybody with half some sense knows it doesn't hardly ever snow in Mississippi. But who says snow has to be cold and wet?

I was soon to find out how snow can come in ways none of us expect.

On Christmas Eve, I went to bed right after supper, dog tired. The grown-ups stayed awake.

Said—their Christmas present to me was to do my chores by cleaning up after our meal. I settled in bed, let a snore take me over.

Mostly, I'm the first one awake at the tiniest glint of morning. But somehow, on Christmas Day, my family beat me to it.

Pa Rollins woke me. Tugged on my toe.

Said, "Aggie, come!"

Not fully roused, I moved slow.

Pa Rollins yanked at my arm. At least he let me sit up and knuckle the sand from out my eyes. Aunt 'Retta was there, too, both of them big smiling. Once I was standing, Pa Rollins steered me to our common room, the place we gathered most as a family.

I blinked, giggled, laughed full-out.

Oh, holy day!

Pa Rollins was clapping, moving foot-to-foot like a happy toad. Together, he and Aunt 'Retta sang a made-up ditty.

White Christmas!
Bright Christmas!
Snow!
Snow!
Snow!

Strung-up cotton bolls, dripping and pretty, rafter to rafter, decorated this day. Strands dotted with dandelions trimmed the whole place, every which way, and winking!

There was a special gift for me. A yellow paper tablet for writing, and two new pencils that even had erasers!

Aunt 'Retta and Pa Rollins folded me in a hug so tight, celebrating the sweet greetings of our very own Mississippi white Christmas.

Pa Rollins took both my and Aunt 'Retta's hands. Whirled all of us together in a giddy dance, Aunt 'Retta using her cane to balance her rhythms. We spun the snow-ditty with happy harmonies.

All of us rejoicing.

The best Christmas gift, though, was that night when Pa Rollins came to my room with a flat present wrapped in a little lacy blanket, decorated with a pine sprig.

Said, "The gift and its wrapping are something I've been saving for you. The lace-lined coverlet is the birth blanket I crafted for you before you were born. What's inside is special. Open it."

When I peeled off the fabric wrapping, it was like looking in a mirror at my own brown-girl skin, proud nose, pillow lips, and black eyes. Her skin had the beautiful hue of a sunflower's center. The spray of freckles dotting high cheekbones were the same as mine, a speckled mix that made me, me. I traced the photograph, curled at its edges, with my thumbs. Nothing missy-miss about that face in the picture. All grit, this woman. Her smile showed a spark of will. Eager, she was.

Pa Rollins told me, said, "Tess, your mama."

I couldn't hardly say something.

I blurted, "She's beautiful and bold, all in the same face."

Pa Rollins nodded.

Said, "Who she look like?"

I didn't need to answer. We both knew who he meant.

Wet came to my father's eyes.

Said, "She loved you fierce, Aggie."

I couldn't help but challenge Pa Rollins.

Said, "Why ain't she here, then?"

Pa Rollins told me, said, "Tess wanted what we call *city different*. She had a hankering for getting far away from Mississippi, to a place with buildings tall enough to poke the clouds. She wanted to take you with her, but I was not having it. On the morning your mama left out from here, she walked to the edge of our land, but had misgivings."

I held close to my mother's photograph.

Pa Rollins kept on.

Said, "Your ma was going toward something she didn't know. We decided it was better to raise you in the heart of our family, right here in Mississippi. Tess left, with no forwarding address. That's because she didn't have a plan for where she'd end up."

An odd kind of empty filled me then. Like losing a tooth, feeling the hole, missing it.

Pa Rollins nodded at the photo.

Said, "Turn it over. Look at the back."

When I did, there was the curled handwriting of some-body who was careful to form letters like they were jewelry.

I read the inscription:

To my Aggie,
Pave your place, precious girl.
My love opens your road.

Pa Rollins, he said, "It's all we have of her."

Somehow, seeing my mother's face, looking so much like mine, was believing in the power of her love for me.

I wrapped the lace blanket back around the picture, tucked it in my pillow slip, near to my marble. Slept, felt bundled, hugged, loved.

A LETTER TO FRIENDS
I HAVE NEVER MET

WHERE AND WHEN: *Ruleville, Mississippi.*
January 1964. Aggie is back at her small family table,
her chair pulled in close. She grips one of her new
pencils, leans hard on her yellow tablet, writing
furiously under the hue of a single bulb.

Dear Cassius Clay and Wilma Rudolph,

If this were a test, there would be six questions.

Have you heard of the five W's and the one H?

Do you know about the Q's and the A's?

Well, here's the big quiz that leads to the same grade.

(Get ready for your homecoming victory parade.)

THE Q's = QUESTIONS.

1. Q. *Who* said it couldn't be done?

2. Q. *What* were you thinking...

3. Q. ...*When* you stepped into the ring and onto the track?

4. Q. *Where* do you go when everybody says *no*?

5. Q. *Why* even try?

6. Q. *How* did you feel when the world said you couldn't, wouldn't, shouldn't, didn't?

THE A's = ANSWERS.

1. Don't give naysayers the time of day.

2. Keep on!

3. Head up!

4. Go 'head!

5. Have to!

6. Can. Will. Should. Do.

GRADE = GOLD +

Sincerely,
Your friend,
Aggie B.

BILLY-CLUB BULLIES

WHERE AND WHEN: *Everyplace in the Magnolia State. The early months of 1964. Aggie works hard to appear strong. But she weakens with this recollection.*

S OMETIMES BETTER AND BITTER KEEP CLOSE COMPANY.

Earning the right to vote gave us hope. But trouble followed soon after.

It was a new year. I was new, too, coming up on the end of being twelve. I joined the Student Nonviolent Coordinating Committee, where I worked alongside Miss Fannie Lou Hamer, who had become one of the SNCC field secretaries in Mississippi. I was one of the youngest SNCC members. Most everyone else was in college, which is where my sights were set for someday. As a SNCC member, I continued to help Colored people in Ruleville and other towns register to vote. I marched. Spoke. Attended voter registration workshops. Spread the word about the unfair registration tests and the poll taxes required to cast a ballot, and helped people older than me learn what all those twisty sentences in the Mississippi law books meant.

Miss Collier, our church organist, asked why, being that I was too young to even go to high school, let alone vote, I was so set on this road.

I told her, said, "Aggie B. is hard-bent on getting Negroes all over the state of Mississippi registered."

I wasn't the only one, either. There were hundreds of kids like me, wanting equality.

Not all of us were SNCC members, but so many still came peacefully, with picket signs and unity songs. Proud people, we were. Townsfolk. Believers. Supporters. Grown-ups and kids, together.

As we made our way, we always knew there was a good chance we'd get arrested. Hauling us off was common. It was like a game for the police. They loved to arrest us, just for fun, it seemed.

When we showed up, out came their handcuffs. In time, the skin on my wrists had toughened up from being bit by those metal clamps.

Our determination brought on all kinds of ugly intolerance, brutality against anybody who dared to stare down injustice.

Hate groups and the police tried to stop us. They harassed adults, mostly, but we kids had a front-row seat to the darkest side of cruel.

My SNCC friends were punched.

Kicked.

Spit on.

Arrested.

Mauled.

Hauled to jail.

Beaten black-and-blue.

Cussed at.

Smacked.

Angry racists attacked with wooden sticks. Billy-Club Bullies, I called them. Some were the police. Others were regular people who'd gotten their hands on one of those hard-hard batons, and just liked hitting. I had been spared mostly, until one day when Billy-Club Bullies found their way to me.

It was the coldest January on record for Mississippi, a Saturday. Pa Rollins was especially busy now, tending to the salted meats that would get us through the rest of winter. Aunt 'Retta rested on Saturdays and Sundays.

I spent my weekends at our school, tutoring grown-ups on how to pass the voting test. I didn't hear the police cars right off. They rolled up quietly onto the grass, dried acorns crunching under thick tires.

It was their headlights reflecting off the windows that blinked a warning. Our teacher, Miss Saunders, told us to gather up, and to quietly make our way to the cellar door, around back. There were only eleven of us, three kids, the rest grown-ups, all we-all students in one way or another. We hurried toward the cellar, but it was too late. A group of police stood at the door blocking it. There were four of them, I think, or maybe more. We joined together, held hands, stood, waited quietly. Our strength seemed to feed the Billy-Club Bullies. Miss Saunders approached, looking like she wanted to say something to the police. But she never got the chance to speak. Billy-Club Bullies moved in like a blizzard.

BAM-BAM-BAM-BAM-BAM-BAM-BAM-BAM!

The batons came down hard. I covered all my head with both arms. Those pounding sticks moved off of me and the other two kids. But for the rest of the folks, the grown-ups, the Billy-Club Bullies kept on and on and *on.* Grizzly bear rain, not letting up, their echo slamming in both my ears.

BAM!

                    BAM!

BAM!

BAM!   *BAM!*

          BAM!   *BAM!*

The pounding took on its own drum-beat storm. Came back again in my direction. I was forced to tuck my whole self inside my whole self. The stick-hits left me pleading through my nosebleeds.

Have mercy!

Haaave mercy!

Ha'…ha'…mercy!

I begged from places deep-deep. Grunted. Snorted. Choked
on the ropes of spit closing off my throat.

BAM! BAM! BAM!

BAM!

BAM! BAM! BAM!

    BAM!

BAM! BAM! BAM! BAM! BAM! BAM!

BAM!

BAM...BAM...BAM...BAM...BAM...BAM...BAM...
BAM! BAM! BAM! BAM! BAM! BAM! BAM!

BAM!

   BAM...BAM...BAM...BAM...BAM...BAM...
BAM...BAM!

  Ha'...mercy! Please!

  Please! Please! Have! Mercy!

    Ha'...ha'...mercy!

But Billy is brutal—*no mercy.*

  BAMBAMBAMBAMBAMBAMBAM!
BAMBAMBAMBAMBAMBAMBAM!!!!

  BAMBAMBAMBAMBAMBAMBAM!
  BAMBAMBAMBAMBAMBAMBAM!

BAMBAMBAMBAMBAMBAMBAM-BAM!!!!

BAMBAMBAMBAMBAMBAMBAM!BAM-BAM-BAM-BAM-BAM-BAM-BAM-BAM!

BAM-BAM-BAM-BAM-BAM-BAM-BAM-BAM!!!!
BAM-BAM-BAM-BAM-BAM-BAM-BAM-BAM!!!!!!!!!!!!!!!!!!!!

BAM-BAM-BAM-BAM-BAM!BAM-BAM-BAM-BAM-BAM-BAM-BAM-BAM!!!BAM-BAM-BAM-BAM-BAM-BAM-BAM-BAM!

BAM-BAM-BAM-BAM-BAM!

Still, I pleaded.

Have…mercy…

Ha'mercy!…

Ha'mercy!   *Haaave…mercy…*

Ha'mercy!…

Have! Mercy!

                    Ha'…mercy !

Shuddered.

The policeman's baton wouldn't quit. That stick! Kept on!

The butt at its end *rammed, rammed, rammed* my ribs. Shattering them like twigs.

Then here comes Dumb Doubt-y, shaking hands with the Billy-Club Bullies, and the two of them fast at work, rattling me.

BAM-BAM-BAM-BAM-BAM-BAM-BAM-BAM!!!!
BAM-BAM-BAM-BAM-BAM-BAM-BAM-BAM!!!!!!!!!!!!!!!!!!!!
BAM-BAM-BAM-BAM-BAM! BAM-BAM-BAM-BAM-BAM-BAM-BAM-BAM!!!
BAM-BAM-BAM-BAM-BAM-BAM-BAM-BAM!

BAM-BAM-BAM-BAM-BAM!

I'm blinded.

My whole face, bloodied.

Numb.

Can't hardly breathe.

Have…Haaave…Ha'…Ha'…mer…merrrr…ceeeeee…!

SEEING STARS

WHERE AND WHEN: *Someplace between here and the other side of tomorrow. Shrill sirens wail. Flashing lights. Red. White. Blue. Aggie is on her knees, buckled over, hugging herself tightly, working hard to breathe. The sirens' moans go quiet. Aggie struggles to speak. This monologue is delivered slowly, deliberately, and with pain. Aggie has been snatched up by the swirl of a delirious fever dream. As her words unfold, the clock's final moments threaten to tell time on the end of Aggie's short life.*

I AM WILMA RUDOLPH, SPRINTING TO A FINISH ONLY I can see.

Neck, chest, even chin, *reaching*, strained to the breaking point, hungry for the win.

My arms ache as they fling behind, letting me lunge, fingers spread wide. Wings extended, lifting me above the powder-dirt.

Dust clouds threaten to choke my throat.

I cough, gag, fight to breathe.

The race turns to a cotton snow blizzard, blustering squalls, a crazy parade of white-on-white—blinding.

My eyes work double time to rake through the glare of *can't-see*.

Like Cassius Clay, I become a grade-A slugger, fighting for what's right.

Is that a book up ahead, pages flapping, waving its words? Clap-clapping, encouraging me to stay in the race, to swing in the ring?

Yes, it's the Mississippi constitution, filled with backward rules and crooked laws that need unlocking to pass the test.

The storm will not let up. Its cold chills my bones, fingertips, toes. That's what happens to this barefooted runner with calloused soles.

But the book, its pages say: *Aggie B., go! Go find answers to the test.*

And so, I race ahead, fists lifted now, the crackle-cold threatening to bite off my okra-toed feet and frost-burned knuckles.

I wince, keep, keep, keep *on.*

Book, look what I can do with my sharp mind.

Add.

Subtract.

Talk back to backward laws.

As my toes and wrists are about to snap off from the cold, I break the rules of Ruleville.

I can even spell *de facto.*

I'm skilled with coin collecting, too. Watch my finger-work gathering a jar full of *In-God-We-Trust.*

Did I mention Dumb Doubt-y is afraid of me?

That's because I talk back to his ghost.

Say—*Boo to you!*

Say—*Step off, jack! I'm here to speak up.*

I'm ready to raise my own lucky hand that can flutter even higher than a butterfly to meet Dumb Doubt-y's lies, face-on.

It's time for real change, not pocket-change collected to pay fake poll taxes.

But am I running *out* of time?

I'm trying with a will to hold off this dark clock.

Bye-bye, Dumb Doubt-y.

I look to the sky and find a wide-open world, ripe with possibilities on this cloudless day.

Me. Parading in a snow-cotton field of faith.

Still, it's cold out here. I'm going numb.

But here comes a bright ball of promise in a firelight sky.

My marble filled with the sun's hope!

My amarillo agate, brave enough to knock Billy-Club Bullies out of the ring.

My family's voices rise, distant echoes, sharing their memories from long ago with me now. Their experiences flash and flicker, pictures sputtering in my mind's eye.

Why do you think they call it boxing cotton?

Do you see my dreams spinning as high as the sun's eyes?

Pave your place, precious girl.

Don't give up five minutes before a miracle happens.

I talk back to the kin-whispers, sass them.

What about every child living in every state of hate?

But wait—are these the glistening hinges of heaven's front door?

Have Billy-Club Bullies' beatings put me down for the count?

Amazing grace, how sweet the sound.

White Christmas! Bright Christmas!

Go tell it on the mountain.

Can't-see's sky is crisp-blue, the color of wonder.

But—this is not nighttime.

But—this is bright afternoon.

But—the butt of Billy-Club Bullies ramming at my ribs makes me see stars in broad daylight.

Tiny blasts flashing behind my eyes.

Swirling. Blazing.

Too many flares to count.

Hundreds of tiny, growing explosions.

Memory-bursts.

Flickers of days. Years. Tears.

Pesticides sprayed, while we work in stifling heat.

Wooden bat-wing batons, pounding me—down, down, down to the ground, blurring my vision, sending those daylight stars shooting into my broken, bloodied face.

How many are there this time?

I can prove to the man with the skinny-stick neck that I'm able to add up the equation for so much evil.

The baton's *thwack* is back.

Sends more stars to decorate this day.

Five-pointed shapes flap in southern breezes.

I don't need to count them this time.

Those stars are counting on me—*one…two…three…*

Their message floats like an angel, murmuring past my pain…*forty-seven…forty-eight…forty-nine…*

Fifty stars on the American flag—not the thirteen on the Confederate rag—tell me I have a right to be here.

But oh, my toes!

The cold won't let up from biting them off, spitting them out, gristle and all.

I hear more kin-whispers from a soft place. A gentle man, humming.

Sweet Aggie B.

This golden-hinged door is not yours.

Not yet, girl-child. Not yet.

You gots to fight back.

Show that natty stuff how tough you are.

Box it. Run the race.

> *Reach!*

Aggie B., bold one.

Time to bring your firelight.

Little tree, strong, tall.

Branches stretching.

Igniting your new day.

Do you see the colors on our horizon?

Red. White. Blue-on-blue.

The work begins now.

Your finish line is this:

Blue is a so-fine color when it's painting the sky.

*Blue is the promise of possibility when it's coming on as
the dawn.*

*Blue is comfort and beauty when its softened threads
weave warmth.*

My eyes settle behind their lids. The wild dream's dance slows, slips away.

Wakefulness rouses my mind. I tremble.

Someone has brought me to my bed.

Its mattress cradles me.

My amarillo agate lights my pillow from underneath. Its gleam brings warmth, healing, comfort. The shimmer calms my breathing, shows me a new view from behind my eyes.

I see my *own* shine. It's the flicker of *me*.

My feet twitch. They're the only part of my whole body not tucked in sheets dampened by delirium.

First thing I see when my eyes slowly open is the wood-beamed ceiling. And so, I speak right to it.

Softly say, *"Ceiling, it's me, Aggie B."*

My toes, all of them restored from this nightmare, have been slipped inside soft sapphire, welcoming me home.

LET MY PEOPLE VOTE!

WHERE AND WHEN: *More Mississippi. 1964. Aggie is centered on her bed, cradling her knees, pulled close, hugging them to her. Blue darkness surrounds.*

HEALING TOOK TIME. I'D SUFFERED A CONCUSSION. THE Billy-Club Bullies had cracked my cheekbone, left me with a swollen eyelid, big as an egg.

Nearly lost my sight, on account of so much swelling.

The beatings left a skin-wound alongside my ear, down my neck and shoulder. An open sore, like someone had snatched off the brown, showed the pink underneath. There were welts, too. And bruises the color of a burnt onion. And, oh, my ribs—two of them broken.

Aunt 'Retta and Pa Rollins nursed me from earliest mornings into long nights. Pa Rollins mixed a salve of camphor and tree gum. Aunt 'Retta gently rubbed the liniment on my welts.

I didn't speak much—couldn't. When a few words came, they got jammed on my tongue. I was just too weak to speak. Mostly, I whimpered from the throbbing, flaring up in every part of me, except for my feet, comforted inside my soft socks.

For weeks after the beatings, Pa Rollins kept me home. He and Aunt 'Retta only let me leave to use the outhouse.

In the middle of night, I suffered tremors and pain so bad I couldn't even blink or chew. You know what kept me from still not wanting to give up?

Cassius and Wilma.

How many swollen days and nights had they gone through?

How many bullies had gotten up their faces and come down hard?

I was now in the thick of my own Night-Deep. Somewhere in the darkness, my voice came, raspy, but sure.

Murmured, "*Billy-Club Bullies, listen good.*"

Whispered, "*Dumb Doubt-y, pay attention.*"

Cried, "*Billy-Club Bullies, do you understand?*"

Wailed, "*Dumb Doubt-y, you hear me?*"

Had to let those stupid two know I was here.

I put it to them nightly, through the blackest hours, until dawn rose. My strength rose, too. Woke one morning before sunup.

Roared, "You can take cracks at my skull, swell my face, break my bones, and shake my confidence. But I will not let you blind the eyesight of my soul!"

It was as if first-light flared up in me, shining truth, proving that *can't see* has a flip side. When morning rises, when a new day dawns, the sun *can see.*

When my strength returned, and my bruises healed, Aunt 'Retta somehow convinced Pa Rollins to let me go back to working with SNCC, so long as she was always there to watch, help, and guide.

Slowly, slowly, with SNCC's help, Colored citizens started to register. White people, and more teenagers even, joined our cause, worked with us to navigate rocks in the road.

When we rode on buses to polling places, we sang "Go Down, Moses."

I changed the words to suit what was happening all around, and taught the Aggie B. version to everybody who was ready for a new way, especially folks who'd been visited by Dumb Doubt-y.

Instead of "let my people go," we now sang it like this:

Go down, Moses
Way down in Egypt land.
Tell ole Pharaoh
To let my people VOTE!

When Israel was in Egypt land
Let my people VOTE!

Oppressed so hard they could not stand.
Let my people VOTE!

I came to be known as Aggie B., the girl who sings for the right to vote.

Now mind you, if Pa Rollins had taught me anything, it was to not be one of those people who goes around with a strut, carrying on, all cocky. But I would not be honest if I didn't admit I liked that people were singing my song, because it meant folks were paying attention to young people and voting rights.

Once I knew my reputation was spreading its rhythm around, and making people take notice of us trying to get Colored citizens to the polls to cast our vote, I came to understand why I was made to suffer through the darkness of Billy-Club Bully brutality. I saw the reason I'd lived through the Night-Deep of so much ugly. What I know is, I was put here to help. I had to go through unthinkable pain so I could be strong enough to help make important changes.

When it came to anything near to equality, freedom, or justice for Colored folks, Mississippi was still a state in a sorry state.

Turns out, Aunt 'Retta and I ended up traveling to places like South Carolina and Louisiana, preaching the word about how to vote. But, seems it was M-i-s-s-i-s-s-i-p-p-i that needed us most.

This was the Little home state. The place that held our hearts, even though there were some bad pieces to it. All we-all had been born into this high-cotton country under Mississippi's liquid sun. And Aunt 'Retta, the only one in our family who voted for the first time, had cast her ballot right here.

M-i-s-s-i-s-s-i-p-p-i was the reason I jumped quick when members of SNCC started to help organize the Mississippi Freedom Democratic Party (MFDP).

The MFDP was ready to help Mississippi climb to a new state of being, so anybody in the Magnolia State could get represented. We had to make our *own* political party, because the regular all-White Mississippi Democratic Party, who called themselves the Regulars, wouldn't invite us to *their* party. It is bad manners to show up when you're not invited. But sometimes you just got to arrive.

The Mississippi Democratic Party didn't allow Colored people in the door, so we made our *own* door, which was wide open to Colored folks, White people, Christians, Jews, or anybody else who wanted to join in the work we were doing at the MFDP.

I guess being mouthy and determined, and talking back to Dumb Doubt-y and the Billy-Club Bullies, was getting us someplace, because I became one of the youngest, and most vocal, volunteers in the MFDP.

The first thing I did to help people who were still afraid to fight for their rights was to let them know that Dumb Doubt-y was fired.

There was no place for uncertainty at *this* party. We were here to celebrate everything that was possible.

I was now a girl who wore socks, yes I did, my favorite being the sapphires that made me strong wherever we walked. Those tall-legged socks held me up, fortified my knees and legs, gave me smart feet.

I worked with a team of young volunteers. Together, we managed to help register thousands of Colored people from M-i-s-s-i-s-s-i-p-p-i into the MFDP. And there were hundreds of kids counting the days for when they'd be old enough to vote, too.

Hundreds and thousands, they are some real big numbers, aren't they?

Well, big was the way we wanted to be.

Our party was just getting started.

THE MFDP AND ME

WHERE AND WHEN: *The Democratic National Convention. Atlantic City, New Jersey, August 1964 and Chicago, Illinois, August 1968. Aggie is seated right behind a table filled with a large group of delegates from Mississippi.*

THERE WE WERE, AUNT 'RETTA AND ME, AND THE MFDP, in front of what must have been a-thousand-and-some people at the Democratic National Convention, in Atlantic City, New Jersey.

Flashbulbs showed off like fireflies at a twinkle contest. News cameras, flags, banners, campaign posters, and VOTE signs covered the walls and halls.

This being up north, I looked deep into the crowds of people hoping that somehow, someway, by some chance of maybe, I would find my mama in here.

I'd brought the picture of her in a small satchel. Kept it close. Tess wasn't anywhere I could see. But she *was* with me on the inside quiet place where forgiveness lives.

Northern states had been my mother's home all these years. She was living free of Jim Crow, and most likely representing Colored people in the best way by showing what it means to live your truth, for you. Wasn't I doing the same thing now, here with Aunt 'Retta, also strong and striking out?

We women were on the same road.

And, *whew-wee*, there were plenty of *we women* here, stepping up on smart feet.

Those signs encouraging people to vote made me shake my head, brought pestering heat to my insides. *We* sure didn't need any convincing. We were there to fight for the right *to* vote.

And don't you know, there was a banner up front, high above all the people and flags that said: LET US CONTINUE.

So all right, then, the Mississippi Freedom Democratic Party—the MFDP and me—we were there *to* continue. More than sixty MFDP delegates had traveled a long way to make them *let us*.

All the thousand-and-some people in that place were there to witness delegates from each state choose the Democratic candidate for president.

The MFDP wasn't the only delegation from Mississippi. The Regulars had come along, too. There was *some* kind of *something* about to happen, only I didn't know full-what.

Here we were, so ready. Gathered together to celebrate democracy. To rejoice in what's fair and right and equal for all people. But the Democratic Party's credentials committee, they would not *let us*, the MFDP, do what we showed up to do. The committee was fixed on the convention rules. They would only allow one group from Mississippi to represent the state.

Didn't they know many were residents of Ruleville, and that rules didn't scare us off, or hold us back? In fact, from living in Ruleville, and knowing what I know, sitting there, I *knew* not to even think twice or again about rules that were stupid.

So here come the Regulars, saying *they* were the *official* ones from Mississippi to represent, and *they* should be the *only* ones from the Magnolia State seated at the convention.

Now how you going to tell me anybody's more *official* than anybody else? The way I see it, every living, breathing creature who's got something to contribute to this world is *officially* allowed to be, and deserves to *be* heard and *be* seen, and *be* seated.

But instead of *letting us continue* with the convention, and *letting* all the delegates from Mississippi have a voice, the credentials committee *let themselves* get all tangled up in senseless rules, and with deciding who was *official*.

And they *let* the news cameras and flashbulbs blind them to what democracy means.

And they *let* the Regulars talk them into believing they were the only delegates who could represent M-i-s-s-i-s-s-i-p-p-i.

And so, the sign that said LET US CONTINUE was a waste of paint.

At least the credentials committee *let us* say our side of things. We had picked Miss Hamer to be one of our spokespeople. Next thing I knew, a microphone on a string was being slipped over her head like a necklace. They tied a contraption around her neck, and insisted she speak slow and clear.

Now, I have been through some hot summers in Mississippi, and even here in New Jersey, there was a simmer working its heat on me, but when all those television cameras with their bright lights came on—when every ear in the room waited to hear our side of things—it made me feel hot in a whole new way. Hot-proud.

Miss Fannie Lou spoke for all of us.

She told. Showed. Testified.

Spoke to the American public about the bloodshed, horror, and humiliation we'd lived through, on account of trying to help Colored citizens register to vote. Took them back to how we traveled to Indianola, and what-all happened afterward.

Aunt 'Retta stomped her cane each time Miss Hamer proclaimed her truths, rocked in her seat, affirming.

When I started remembering the hard-crack of billy clubs, something got choked in my throat. I had to fight it off so I could listen better. Somehow when trying-not-to-cry gets stuck in the wayback of your tongue, it makes it hard to pay attention.

Every bone and muscle in my healed-up body worked to keep from crying. I was there to be strong. Didn't want to crack, for fear I would bust open and turn into a puddle. What good would that do? Believe me, I got nothing against being true to a feeling, but I needed to save welling up for later.

I was thankful for Miss Fannie Lou's microphone necklace then. Hearing her voice coming through so loud and strong helped me stay focused while she spoke.

Told—how we'd suffered.

Said—how we'd been shut out of the voting polls.

Showed what Billy-Club Bully brutality can do. Testified about hatred and pain. Spoke for so many of us. Described the tangle of emotions that had gotten all knotted-up inside me. In my heart's eye, I saw Pa Rollins, who, through all of this, stayed back in Ruleville. I felt the deep daughter-love for my father, who had allowed his only child to walk this scary path, away from him, toward a hidden tomorrow. Aunt 'Retta must have felt this same heart-tug. She stomp-stomped her cane with a sure rhythm. *Ca-gung! Ca-gung!*

That's what did it. Like sudden rain, here come my tears. As much as I tried to hold them back, they were turning them camera lights and flashbulbs into bright blurs. I squeezed my toes inside my socks to hold myself together.

Miss Fannie Lou ended her testimony with a charge.

Declared, "All of this is on account of we want to register, to become first-class citizens. And if the Freedom Democratic Party is not seated now, I question America."

She brought home her point with a question. A *de facto* question. It was real!

Thundered, "Is this America, the land of the free and the home of the brave, where we have to sleep with our telephones off the hook because our lives be threatened daily, because we want to live as decent human beings, in America?"

I took a heavy breath.

Seems everybody else was holding on to *their* breath, too, afraid to let it loose, and was silent and wondering what would happen next.

The telephones at the credentials committee headquarters started ringing and ringing, with people all calling. Voices urgent. Putting it to the committee *to let* the MFDP delegation be seated.

How hard would that have been? But no, they couldn't just *let us continue*. Instead, the committee came ahead with a compromise.

Said—the MFDP could be unofficial delegates.

Told us—*two* of our sixty-something who'd traveled all

this way could be seated with *all* of the delegates from the Regulars.

Well, by then, I didn't have any more tears choking my throat or robbing my ears. Like everyone else in the MFDP, I was there to bring my purpose. I was as determined as the rest of them to make a change. Aunt 'Retta's cane was doing triple time. *Ca-gung-ca-gung-ca-gung!* Beating out angry protests.

My feet, smarter than ever, stomped, too, just as fast, twice as loud. *Ga-gonk-ga-gonk-ga-gonk!*

To *let* our presence be seen again, each and every one of us stood up. Aunt 'Retta didn't need my help, or her cane even. She hooked it on the arm of her chair.

Two seats was not enough. We were fed up, and so were the other delegates who had come all this way.

But our determination didn't pierce through the committee's indifference. We returned to the convention two more nights after that, still proud to be members of the MFDP. And do you think they *let us* all be seated? No. They'd gone on to whatever came next, and so did we. Boarded our bus, went back to Mississippi, uncertain about what to do.

When we left New Jersey, the only thing we knew for sure was that Lyndon B. Johnson had been nominated to run for president on the Democratic ticket. But, as far as we were concerned, there was no kind of *democratic* anything looking out for the rights of the MFDP.

Also, later, come to find out Lyndon B. Johnson had tried to pull attention away from our group that was shining a light on so many injustices. That man who would soon be running for president had called all the television networks with what he said was an emergency press conference. He was hoping to distract them, so they would turn their cameras from the MFDP to him. Yes, this truly happened. But the only real emergency was the siren of segregation ringing its truth by the all-together voice of our presence.

As much as Lyndon B. tried, all eyes were *not* on him. Turns out, a whole lot of television stations ended up putting Miss Fannie Lou's speech and our work with the MFDP ahead of whatever *emergency* that man had tried to scrounge up.

After seeing what-all happened on TV, our MFDP membership grew. We joined forces with other organizations that were part of a larger group that some folks called the Mississippi Loyalist Democratic Party. Others called them the Loyal Democrats of Mississippi or just the Mississippi Loyalists. All these names fit like a sturdy pair of dungarees. And all of them spoke to being *loyal*. That's what mattered to me most—staying true to this cause.

Even some of the Regulars joined our group.

Four years later, we traveled to the Democratic National Convention in Chicago, Illinois. Told them we were back with more members, Colored people and White folks, committed to change.

Being at that convention a second time was like hearing words repeat on a record when the needle is caught in a groove.

In Chicago, the credentials committee was stuck on their same song. Played it just like they did in Atlantic City. When we asked to all be seated to represent our state along with the Regulars, the committee tried to weasel out of it. Again.

We refused. Again.

I was a full-on teenager now. Still too young to vote, but more grown from when we'd traveled to Atlantic City.

Aside from loud, we were persistent. Being older, I saw things differently. Knowing how Pa Rollins's doggedness had got him through his Night-Deep and mine, and so much else that kept our family strong, I'd learned there is no shame in what some people might consider stubborn. Hardheadedness is a good thing when you're holding fast to what's right. To me, *that's* loyalty. This was especially true on that evening. After all I had endured, my skull was thick. My backbone, solid. My commitment more firm than ever.

By then, we'd said everything we needed to say to the committee, so all us delegates, we just waited. Stayed stubborn. Stayed strong. *Stayed*.

Finally, we were all seated. Me. Aunt 'Retta and the rest of us loyal and true folks, there to make a difference.

You know how I do. Aggie B. likes the front row, first seat, best view. On that night, from where I sat, I could see justice up close.

Soon as Miss Fannie Lou Hamer lowered herself into her *official* seat, everybody else on the convention floor stood up. Gave her an ovation!

And, oh, how my tears flowed.

They came hard and quick.

It was joy-crying!

AFTER THE AFTER

She returns on the blurred horizon,
comes up the road
hoisting a shiny patent leather satchel.

Sure-footed,
confident,
expectant,
eager.

Make no mistake.

Those are smart feet
filling new shoes.

Pa Rollins
        greets her with a marigold bouquet.

Aunt 'Retta
        brings sweet tea.

Aggie B.,
>   close behind, approaches,
>   her whole heart pumping
>   when she sees that smile!

>   Mama!

This well-heeled lady,
this mother-come-home,
reveals what's in her bag.

Proudly shows off the treasures filling her satchel.

A cap and gown.
A rolled diploma.
A degree.

Tess Coles Little,
now a happy college graduate!

She's been educated in up-north classrooms,
a music student who's come into her own.

She's perfected smooth piano.
She's learned to read music spelled out
  on university blackboards.

And now, she's returned
to help change the out-of-tune rules of Ruleville.

She needed to chase that wind-song
to reach her people
with newfound know-how.
And now,
this lady
is back for good.

Here
to play a whole new refrain.

Here
to let us hear melodies that stride with promise.

Here
to stay.

Here
to prove we've passed a hard-won test.

The test of waiting,
wanting,
wondering
what comes next.

Smart feet return
to plant more legacy seeds
at the base of their Golden Tree.

The Littles hold their faces
toward the horizon of a glistening sun.

Hold their gazes to the light.

One family, shining bright.

> *Reunited.*
> *Rising.*

SAID AND DONE

WHERE AND WHEN: *A wide-open field decorated
with Mississippi magnolia trees. Aggie, Pa Rollins, and
Aunt 'Retta have gathered, their feet solidly planted. Aggie
starts with fists clenched at her sides, but soon her body
loosens. Pa Rollins holds a bouquet of just-picked wildflowers.
Aunt 'Retta is seated in a rocking chair between them,
relaxed, reflecting. As this final tri-monologue unfolds, each
character's eyes and hands reach toward the sky.
They're exuberant. Triumph flows.*

Aunt 'Retta

When people remember things, they say it's like something happened yesterday. But I think upon it different. To me, this time of recollecting is like celebrating what's happening tomorrow.

Because tomorrow is when the new day is comin' *on*.

Tomorrow, when hope's risin' up, is where my eyes are cast.

And when it comes time for me to walk through the door with the glistening hinges, and they ask if there's anything I wish I'd done before I got there, I'll say—*more*.

Aggie B.

My eye is on what's happening next.

On freedom.

On hope.

On the vote.

Me, I'm just one small piece of a big dream.

There was James, and Charles, who got us started by breaking the rules of Ruleville.

PA ROLLINS

There were hundreds of proud, hardworking sharecroppers, clerks, clergy, and kids, living in hardship's grip who broke past the clutched fist of indifference. Well, *uh-huh*, then, I was one of them.

AGGIE B.

Me too, no longer a motherless child.

And there was my Pa Rollins, stubborn in what it means to have a father's love, who saw fit to step aside and let his only child do what she needed to do.

There was Aunt 'Retta, bringing me along for the ride, so that today we walk proudly into tomorrow with heads up and voting ballots in each of our hands.

There was Fannie Lou Hamer, who kept us going with her fortitude.

To make that possible—what truly moved us ahead—was all those feet marching to the polls. *Reaching.*

AUNT 'RETTA

Women and men who'd built their strength from boxing cotton.

Hardworking people who gained a clear vision from so many days and nights and years-upon-years of backbreaking labor in the heat of *can't-see*.

But in time, we *did* see.

Came to know that nobody's free until everybody's free.

Our freedom grew from so many determined souls who passed book-tests, and faith-tests, and how-long-can-we-wait tests.

Our liberty sprung from strong-willed citizens. Obstinate. Not stepping down. Or back.

AGGIE B.

And so, thanks to them, we vote.

We vote for justice.

We vote to overcome.

With democracy leading the way, we *go*. We register.

We *show up*. And *speak up* by casting our voices with our ballots in democracy's box.

By campaigning.

And polling.

And rolling past Dumb Doubt-y.

AUNT 'RETTA, PA ROLLINS, AGGIE B.

We don't ever give up.

AUNT 'RETTA

So name it what you want. Call this *oration*. Truth-talking. Preaching. Speechifying. Testimony. Recollection.

AGGIE B.

Say whatever will inspire *you* to stand up and speak your own truth. Even if words or tears stick in your throat, or you have a hard time stepping past rocks in the road.

PA ROLLINS

Please remember there's a miracle coming in five minutes, or maybe more. But it *is* on the way. If progress is too slow for you, use that wait-time wisely.

AUNT 'RETTA

When you believe in something, go-tell-it.

AUNT 'RETTA, PA ROLLINS, AGGIE B.

Reach for your firelight. Then *go do.*

The Littles exit, walking off on determined feet, smart feet, humming the final notes of a melody. Loretta pauses. Gives a single up-nod. Pa Rollins sniffs his bouquet. Aggie B. reveals her namesake marble. Shows it off, balancing the glowing glass on her palm. Its bold light flares brightly. Blackout.

Go-Tell-It

THIS STORY IS A WORK OF FICTION INSPIRED BY THE COLLEC-
tive voices of many. These first-person narratives are crafted
from interviews and oral histories culled from individuals who
lived under the sharecropping system in the American South
from the 1920s through the late 1960s, some of them members of my very own family.

Though presented as three stories, the imaginary lives and
times of the Little family illuminate the true experiences of
thousands who sought equality during America's era of segregation that led to the social activism set forth during the
civil rights movement.

Stemming from the real-life experiences of these individuals, these first-person recollections are delivered in the
oral storytelling tradition. The tales dramatize the hardships
and triumphs experienced by those living in a society rid-
dled with discrimination and dominated by oppressive forces.

Loretta Little Looks Back: Three Voices Go Tell It is a story of courage and survival that weaves actual events with the emotional truths of those who triumphed over bigotry. Drawing connections to history, several real-life figures are referenced in the monologues. They are Emmett Till, boxer Cassius Clay, who later changed his name to Muhammad Ali, and track runner Wilma Rudolph. Charles McLaurin, James Forman, Fannie Lou Hamer, President Lyndon B. Johnson, and Martin Luther King Jr. are also real figures.

Select events and organizations are historically accurate, including the poisoning of farm animals by racist people seeking to destroy the hopes of African American farmers, voter registration drives, the bus trip from Ruleville to Indianola, the Mississippi Freedom Democratic Party, and the events of the Democratic National Conventions of 1964 in Atlantic City, New Jersey, and in Chicago, Illinois, in 1968, as well as the Olympic triumphs of Cassius Clay and Wilma Rudolph. The voter registration test questions that appear in the story are a composite drawn from actual tests administered to African Americans in various southern states such as Mississippi and Louisiana.

The terms "Colored" and "Negro" are used to refer to

African Americans. These terms were how Americans of African descent referred to themselves, and how people of other races also referred to African Americans during the time frames in which this story is set.

In crafting the narrative sections that depict and reference multiple sclerosis, I was very pleased to work closely with the National Multiple Sclerosis Society to gather information on accurate and sensitive descriptions, as well as historical context. Multiple sclerosis is a common disease of the nervous system whose symptoms began to be identified as early as the 1800s. It was given its medical name much later. While young 'Retta and her doctor may not have known the proper name of the disease, its symptoms and diagnosis would have been identified at that time. For the sake of clarity, I've named the condition in the story.

Certain folkloric aspects of the Little family's life and times are phenomena of my imagination, though drawn from oral histories and storytellings, and presented for their dramatic effects. These include the songs and poems that are not otherwise cited as traditional spirituals, the Golden Angel Cypress tree, the Night-Deep, the sudden summer hailstorm, strange grapes, and the family's magical lighted marble. Agate marbles come in many bright colors. While an "amarillo agate" is not an official name, it is used here to celebrate the power, beauty, and mysticism of a golden ball of glass that ignited the Little family's hope for a bright future and kept their legacy's firelight alive!

—*Andrea Davis Pinkney*

THE DRAMATIC FORM

DELIVERED AS A SERIES OF MONOLOGUES, *Loretta Little Looks Back: Three Voices Go Tell It* is a novel with the intention of inviting readers to step into the shoes of characters, and to experience history through the eyes of those whose life and times represent the resilience of a people.

This novel takes a page-to-stage approach that dramatizes the limits of children living under the lash of oppression. Here, they weave aspects of those times, spanning 1927 to 1968, into vignettes, presenting these as a series of back-to-back long-form monologues. When laced together, these create an affecting story of each individual's experiences, while revealing the emotions surrounding them. Oration brings blood, bone, and breath to the narrative. It is meant to be interactive, to provide read-aloud opportunities, and to bring the past alive with power. Language and speech patterns, drawn from interviews, written accounts, broadcasts, and live performances, provide the cadence for the inflections of the narratives.

As an author and parent, I've discovered that young readers learn best when they connect content to meaning. If they can *feel* what they're reading, they enjoy it to a greater degree, and retain it more readily. Narratives presented in a dramatic fashion provide that opportunity.

The dialogues in this book can be read sequentially or randomly. They can be enjoyed silently, or delivered aloud. The use of time, setting, and action designations help contextualize each vignette.

These monologues, accessed by pulling back an invisible curtain, reveal an intimate portrait of grit and bravery that I hope will inspire young readers to act.

ARTIST'S NOTE

A THEATRICAL APPROACH TO STORYTELLING PRESENTS WONDER-
ful possibilities for an artist. When Loretta Little greeted me
through her brassy narrative, followed by young Roly and his
determined kindness, then by Aggie B.'s grit, I was immediately
drawn in by the visual opportunities this unique format allows.

I concluded that I could best punctuate the emotional
resonance of the recollections through the use of metaphor.

To bring the dialogues into greater dramatic focus, I drew
inspiration from the gels used in theatrical lighting that bring
dimension and emotion to settings and to characters as they
deliver their lines.

I sought to achieve a vivid intensity to the depictions with
paintings rendered in sepia acrylic and India ink, on Srath-
more Watercolor Paper.

These grained art papers have a textural quality to them,
which inspired me to create images that are both conceptual
and expressive.

The testimonies are illuminated through the bold calligraphic strokes of my da Vinci Maestro paintbrushes, paired with the softer lines rendered by the quills of my Japanese sumi brushes.

Each and every time I read Andrea's delivery of Loretta's narrative, I was taken with the fact that Loretta is a knowing soul, the all-wise storyteller whose presence appears across generations and periods of history. And so, in rendering Loretta for the novel's cover, I've sought to capture her probing gaze, which draws strength from the resilience of those who came before her, while at the same time looks ahead into the eyes of hope. Loretta has perspective *and* vision. This is what makes Loretta's story—and the tales of her family members— relevant and necessary for any kid today who cares deeply about others, about drawing strength from people who love you, and making the world a better place for everyone who will follow the path you set. That's what her face says to young readers who first meet her on this book's jacket.

The Little family presents mighty examples of folks who grow strong through their circumstances. By combining expressive paint techniques on the pages of this book and on its cover, I hope to strike empathy in the hearts of readers.

—*Brian Pinkney*

OF DIGNITY AND HARVEST MOONS: SHARECROPPERS IN THE AMERICAN SOUTH

LORETTA'S, ROLY'S, AND AGGIE'S ACCOUNTS REPRESENT THE stories of many sharecroppers who endured an unfair system in which a landowner lets a family use his property in return for a share of the crops they harvest. While this seems to be an equitable arrangement, sharecroppers were often beholden to their landowners, which prevented them from securing their own land, livestock, and crops. Sharecroppers worked long, backbreaking hours, and were sometimes cheated by landowners who promised wages that were never paid. Some dishonest farmers manipulated the scales on which harvested fruits, vegetables, cotton, and other crops were weighed, so that the sharecroppers' work was undervalued, and they were forced to keep picking to "earn" their keep. By working toward voting equality, people  like the Littles and others fought to empower sharecroppers. The folks pictured here could have been their neighbors, friends, and fellow activists. Day after day, and season to season, they worked with their hands, and kept their eyes fixed to what they hoped would be a brighter tomorrow.

THOSE WHO SET THE STAGE

LORETTA LITTLE LOOKS BACK: THREE VOICES GO TELL IT

INCLUDES THESE REAL-LIFE NOTABLES.

CHARLES McLAURIN

Charles McLaurin was a well-spoken crusader who became a friend and supporter of Fannie Lou Hamer, working alongside her to gain justice for African Americans.

EMMETT TILL

Emmett Till was a fourteen-year-old boy who was lynched after being accused of offending a White woman in a grocery store. His brutal death is believed by some to be the spark that ignited the Civil Rights Movement.

JAMES FORMAN

Civil rights pioneer James Forman was a member of the Student Nonviolent Coordinating Committee (SNCC), known for organizing and bringing people together under a common cause.

MARTIN LUTHER KING, JR.

A minister and activist, Martin Luther King Jr. believed in peaceful protests as a way to foster compassionate social action. He was one of the most notable leaders of the Civil Rights Movement.

PRESIDENT LYNDON B. JOHNSON

Often referred to by his initials, LBJ, Lyndon B. Johnson was the thirty-sixth president of the United States.

FANNIE LOU HAMER

A trailblazing woman who spoke up for voting equality, Fannie Lou Hamer inspired many through her civil rights activism. She successfully rallied hundreds of African Americans to register to vote.

Here is my father's family, the Davises, who worked land in the state of Virginia. 'Retta is based on my great-aunt Skip, the girl on the farthest left, white dress. Roly is drawn from my uncle Charlie, the boy in the front row, center. Aggie B. is a composite of my aunt Katherine, the girl on the right center, and my mother, Gwen, not pictured here.

FOR FURTHER READING
AND SHARING

BOOKS:

Adelman, Bob, and Charles Johnson. *Mine Eyes Have Seen: Bearing Witness to the Struggle for Civil Rights.* New York: Time Home Entertainment, 2007.

Brooks, Maegan Parker, and Davis W. Houck, Eds. *The Speeches of Fannie Lou Hamer: To Tell It Like It Is.* Jackson, Mississippi: University Press of Mississippi, 2010.

Carson, Clayborne. *In Struggle: SNCC and the Black Awakening of the 1960s.* Cambridge: Harvard University Press, 1981, pages 124–25.

Carson, Clayborne, David J. Garrow, Gerald Gill, Vincent Harding, Darlene Clark Hine. *The Eyes on the Prize Civil Rights Reader.* New York: Viking Penguin, 1991.

DeMuth, Jerry. "Fannie Lou Hamer: Tired of Being Sick and
Tired." *Nation*, June 1, 1964. Reprinted in *Reporting Civil
Rights: Part Two: American Journalism 1963–1973*. New York:
Penguin, 2003, pages 99–106.

Hamer, Fannie Lou. *To Praise Our Bridges: An Autobiography*.
Jackson, Mississippi: KIPCO, 1967.

Hansen, Joyce. *Women of Hope: African Americans Who Made a
Difference*. New York: Scholastic Press, 1998.

ACKNOWLEDGMENTS

IT IS WITH GRATITUDE THAT I WISH TO THANK THE FOLLOW-ing individuals and institutions who contributed their time and expertise in bringing this novel to light.

I'm grateful to the University of Southern Mississippi and Shenandoah University for providing oral history recordings of sharecroppers, spanning decades, that provided colorful accounts of Mississippi's history, lore, colloquialisms, and cultural references that informed this story.

Thank you to researcher/copy editor Maya Frank-Levine and Jonathan A. Noyalas, director of Shenandoah University's McCormick Civil War Institute, for your invaluable scholarly reads, fact-checking, and contributions to the manuscript. Thanks, too, to Julie Fiol, MSW, BSN, RN, MSCN, Director, MS Information and Resources at the National Multiple Sclerosis Society, for your careful vetting, sensitivity read, and clarification about the symptoms, portrayal, and medical history of multiple sclerosis.

For her expertise in curating the historical photographic images that appear in the back of the book, I wish to thank photo researcher Emily Teresa.

Special gratitude to the creative teams at Chicago's Northlight Theatre and Atlanta's Alliance Theater, for showing me how the power of a page-to-stage narrative can breathe life into a work for children.

Every novel takes a village to create, and I've been blessed with a village of hardworking visionaries at Little, Brown Books for Young Readers. Thank you to my brilliant editor Alvina Ling for seeing the firelight in this book, and for bringing her editorial spark to each and every page. Thank you to the many hands who carried the Little family's story to publication—the eagle eyes of editorial assistant Ruqayyah Daud, production editor Annie McDonnell, and the creative genius of art director Sasha Illingworth, designer Jenny Kimura, and production manager Lillian Sun, whose expertise have delivered this book's beautiful design and package.

Gratitude goes to those who continue to put this book into the hands of readers, the tireless marketing and publicity team at Little, Brown: Alex Kelleher-Nagorski, Michelle Campbell, and the unstoppable Victoria Stapleton.

I am so thankful to my amazing agent, Rebecca Sherman,

whose keen eyes keep the light shining in so many places. Thanks, too, to Alexandra Levick at Writers House, who keeps all trains running happily.

To my cousins Theresa Ransey and Francelia Emanuel Newman, our family historians, I am grateful for continuing to celebrate the names, faces, and roots of our family tree.

And finally, deepest gratitude goes to my husband, Brian Pinkney, who for thirty years has held my hand and my heart, and whose powerful paintings throughout this book bring power, drama, dignity, and vision to the Little family and their triumphs.

More powerful and inspiring stories from
New York Times bestselling author
ANDREA DAVIS PINKNEY

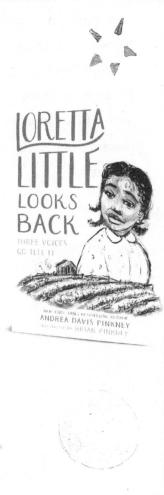

LITTLE, BROWN AND COMPANY
BOOKS FOR YOUNG READERS